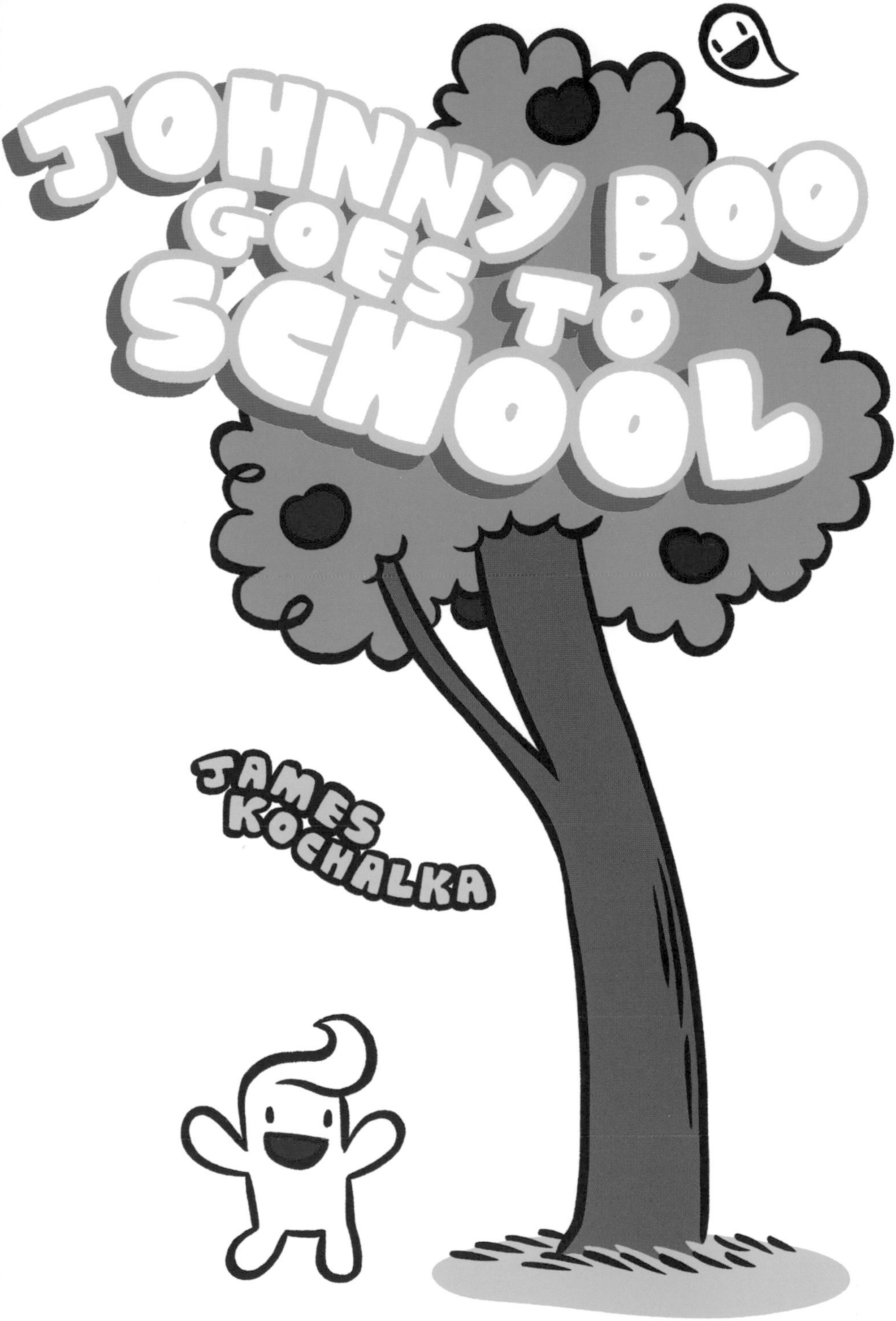
JOHNNY BOO
GOES TO
SCHOOL
JAMES
KOCHALKA

TOP SHELF PRODUCTIONS

An apple for Eli...

...who GRADUATED!

Johnny Boo Goes to School © 2022 James Kochalka.

Published by Top Shelf Productions, an imprint of IDW Publishing, a division of Idea and Design Works, LLC. Offices: Top Shelf Productions, c/o Idea & Design Works, LLC, 2765 Truxtun Road, San Diego, CA 92106. Top Shelf Productions®, the Top Shelf logo, Idea and Design Works®, and the IDW logo are registered trademarks of Idea and Design Works, LLC. All Rights Reserved. With the exception of small excerpts of artwork used for review purposes, none of the contents of this publication may be reprinted without the permission of IDW Publishing. IDW Publishing does not read or accept unsolicited submissions of ideas, stories, or artwork.

Editor-in-Chief: Chris Staros.

Edited by Leigh Walton.

Designed by Nathan Widick.

Visit our online catalog at www.topshelfcomix.com.

Printed in China.

ISBN 978-1-60309-503-7   25 24 23 22   4 3 2 1

CHAPTER ONE

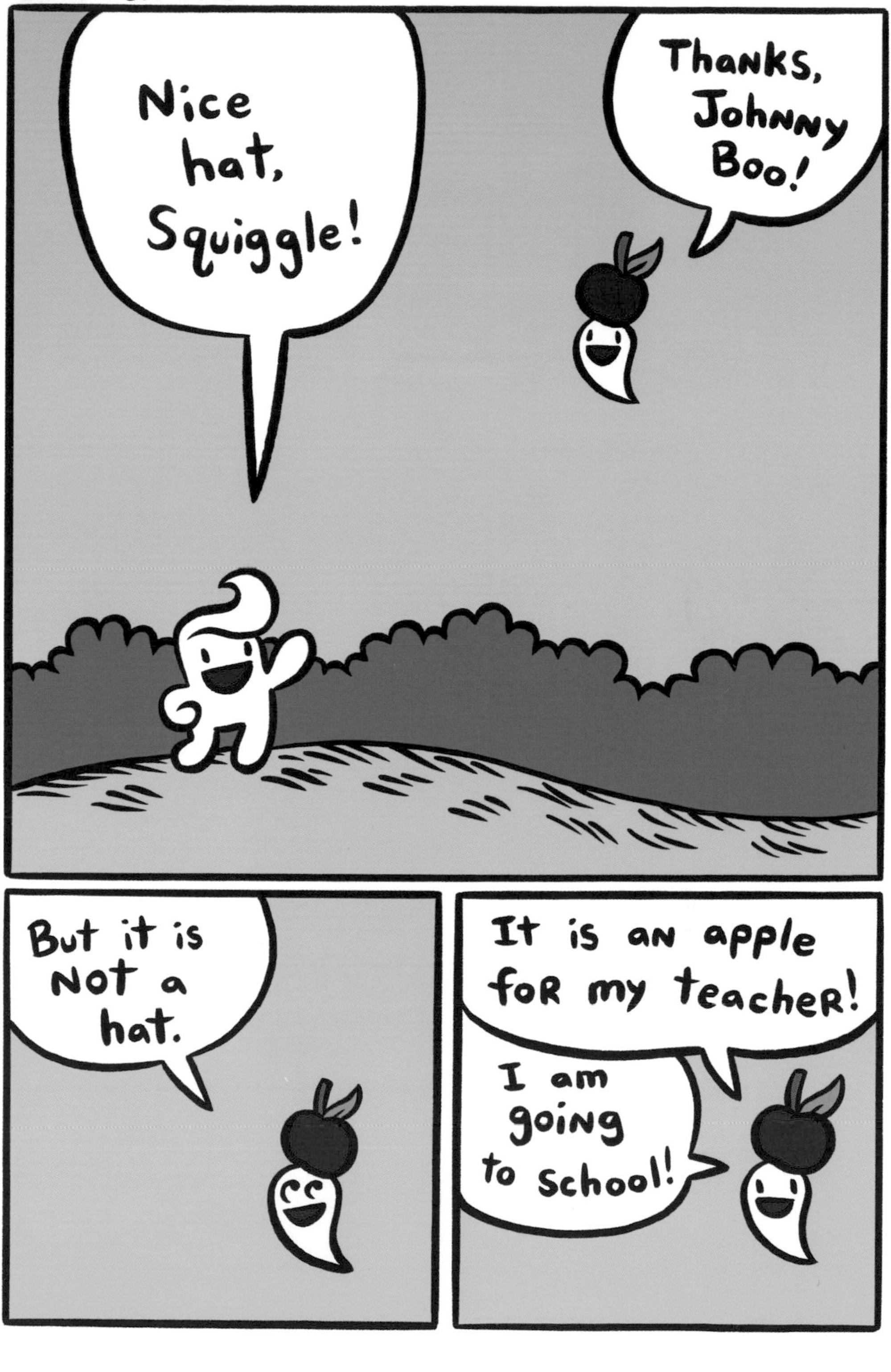
Nice hat, Squiggle!
Thanks, Johnny Boo!
But it is Not a hat.
It is an apple for my teacher!
I am going to school!

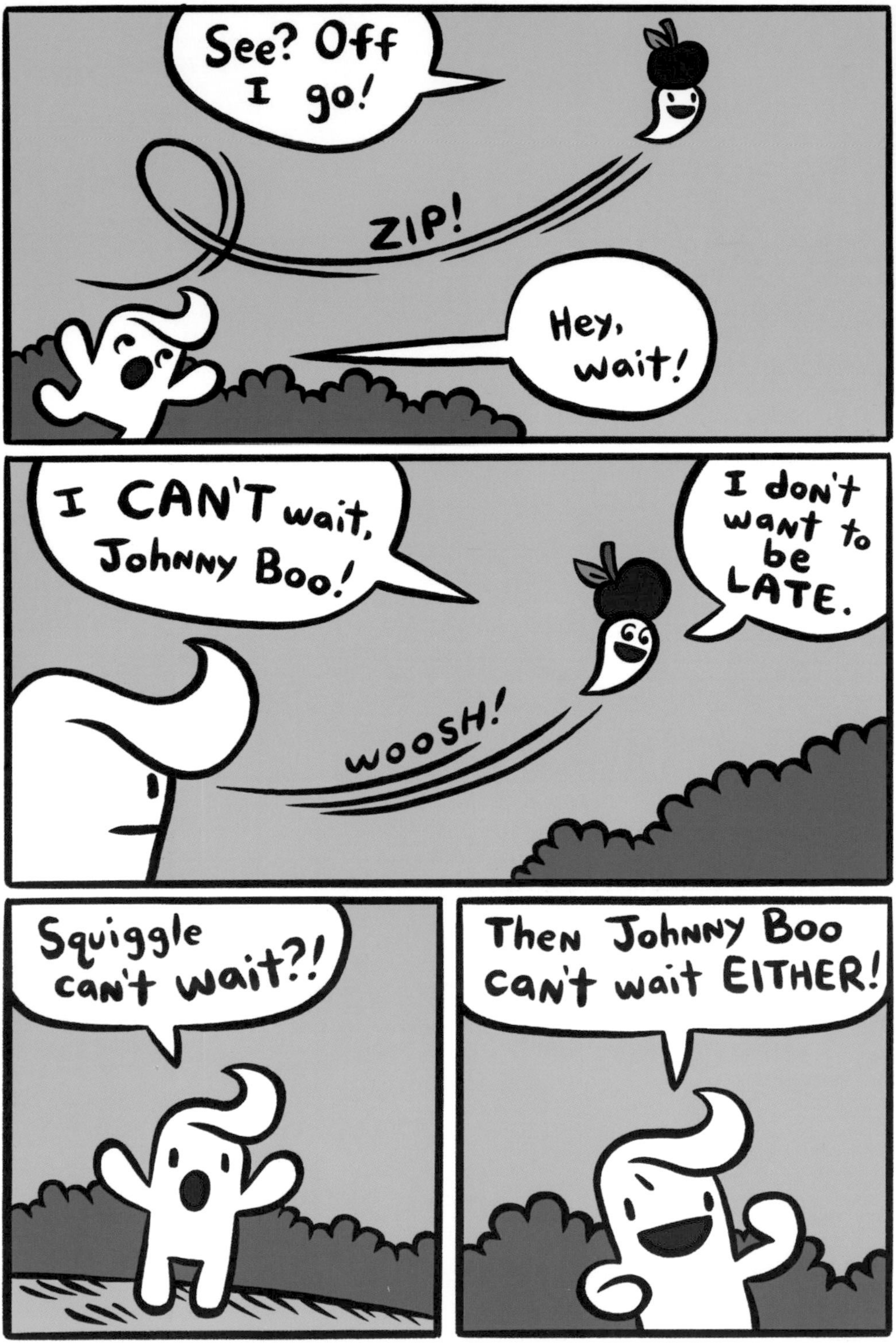
See? Off I go!
ZIP!
Hey, wait!
I CAN'T wait, Johnny Boo!
I don't want to be LATE.
WOOSH!
Squiggle can't wait?!
Then Johnny Boo can't wait EITHER!

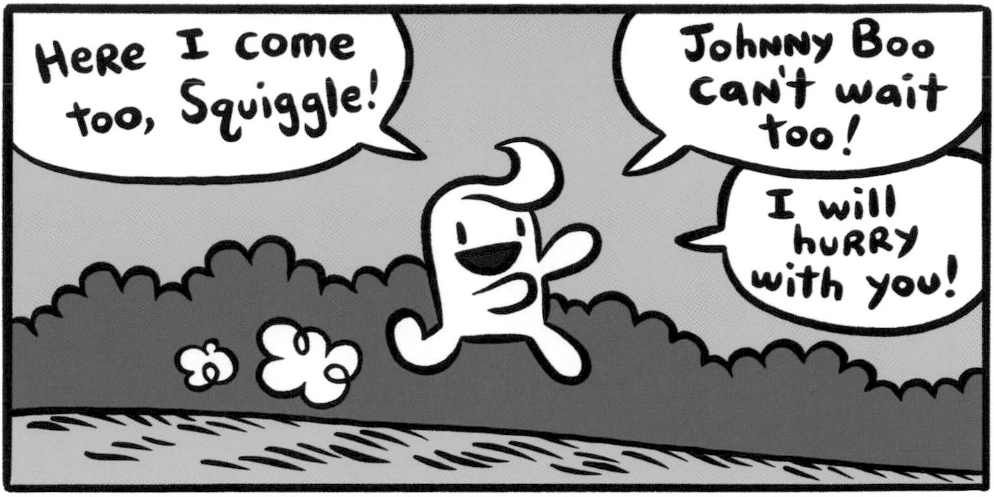

Here I come too, Squiggle!
Johnny Boo can't wait too!
I will hurry with you!

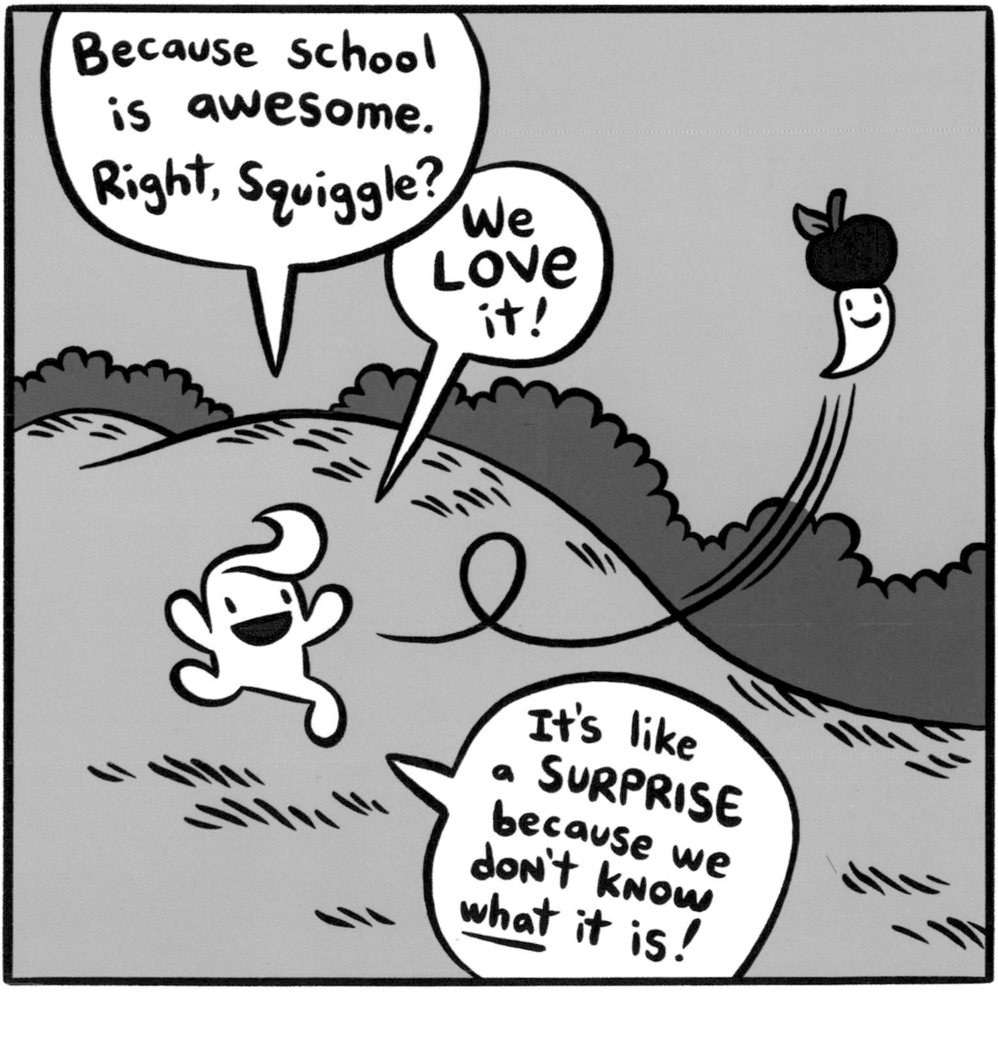

Because school is awesome. Right, Squiggle?
We LOVE it!
It's like a SURPRISE because we don't know what it is!

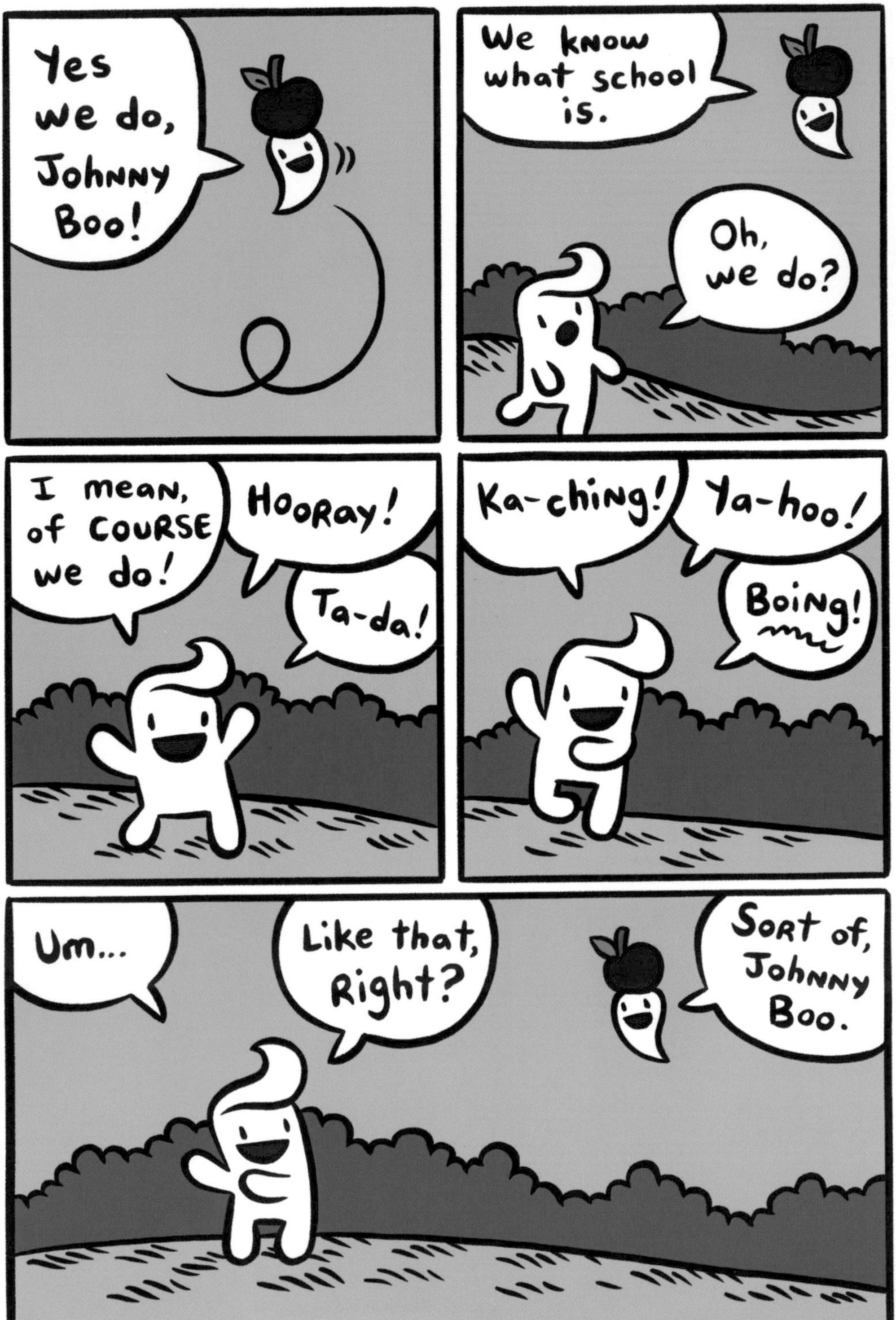
Yes we do, Johnny Boo!
We know what school is.
Oh, we do?
I mean, of COURSE we do!
HOORAY!
Ta-da!
Ka-ching!
Ya-hoo!
Boing!
Um...
Like that, Right?
Sort of, Johnny Boo.

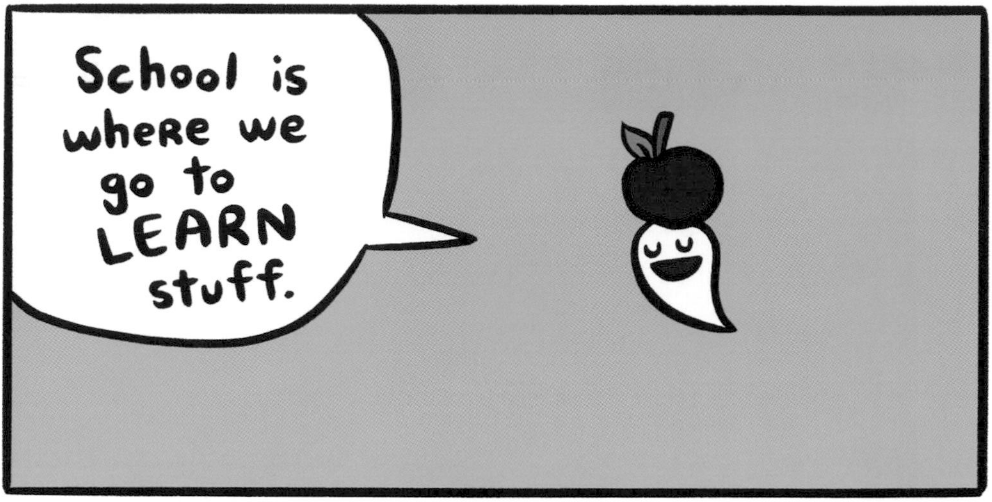
School is where we go to LEARN stuff.

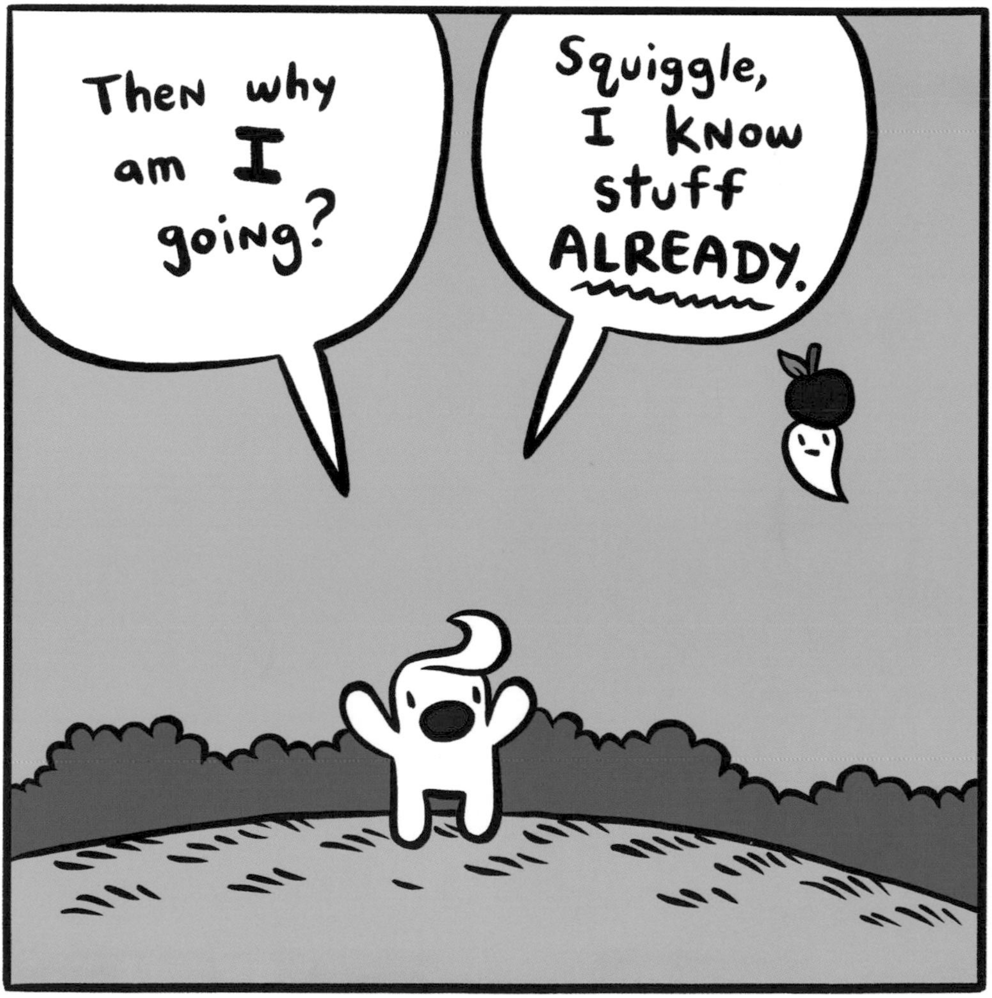
Then why am I going?
Squiggle, I know stuff ALREADY.

CHAPTER TWO

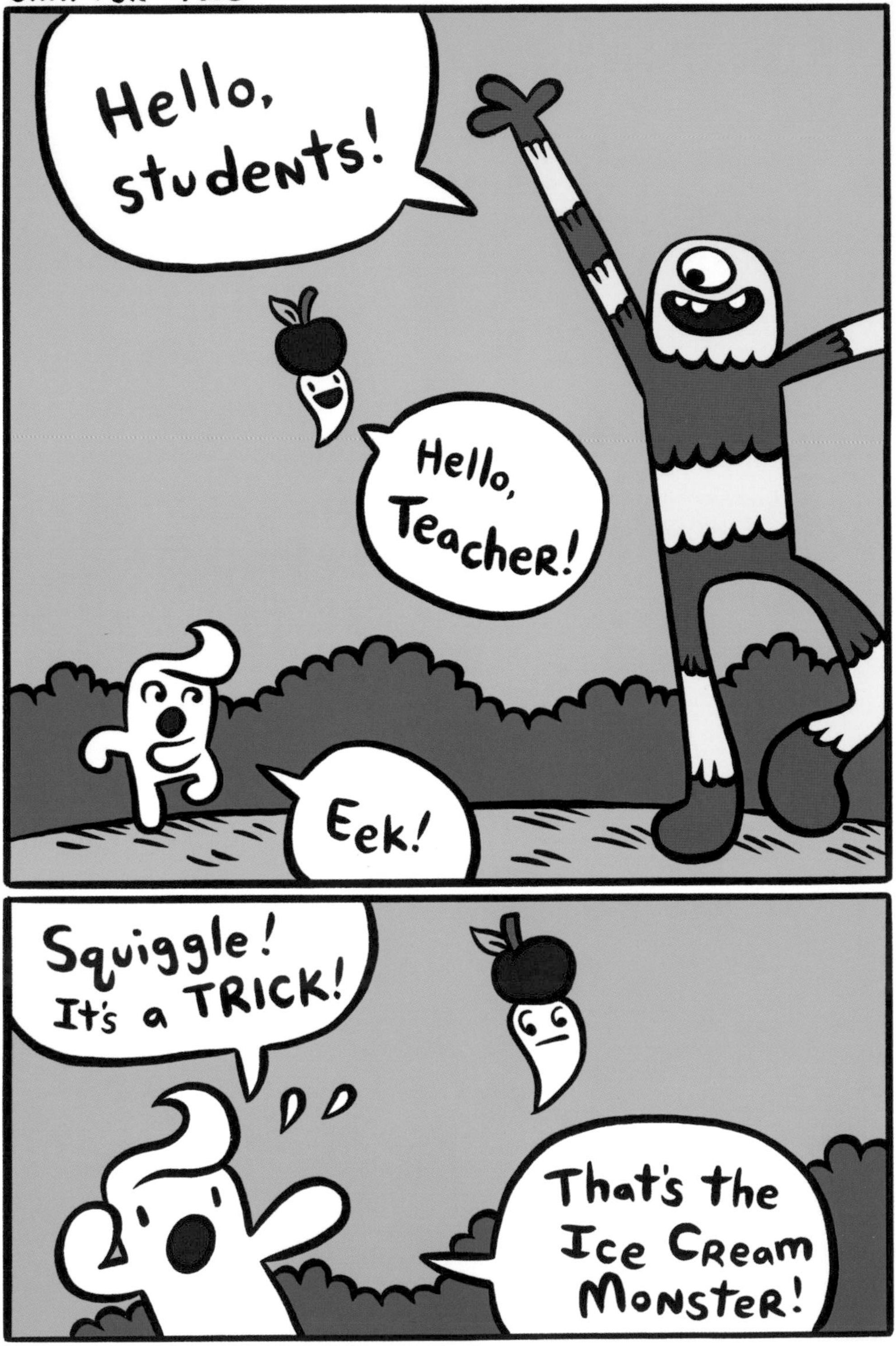
Hello, students!
Hello, Teacher!
Eek!
Squiggle! It's a TRICK!
That's the Ice Cream Monster!

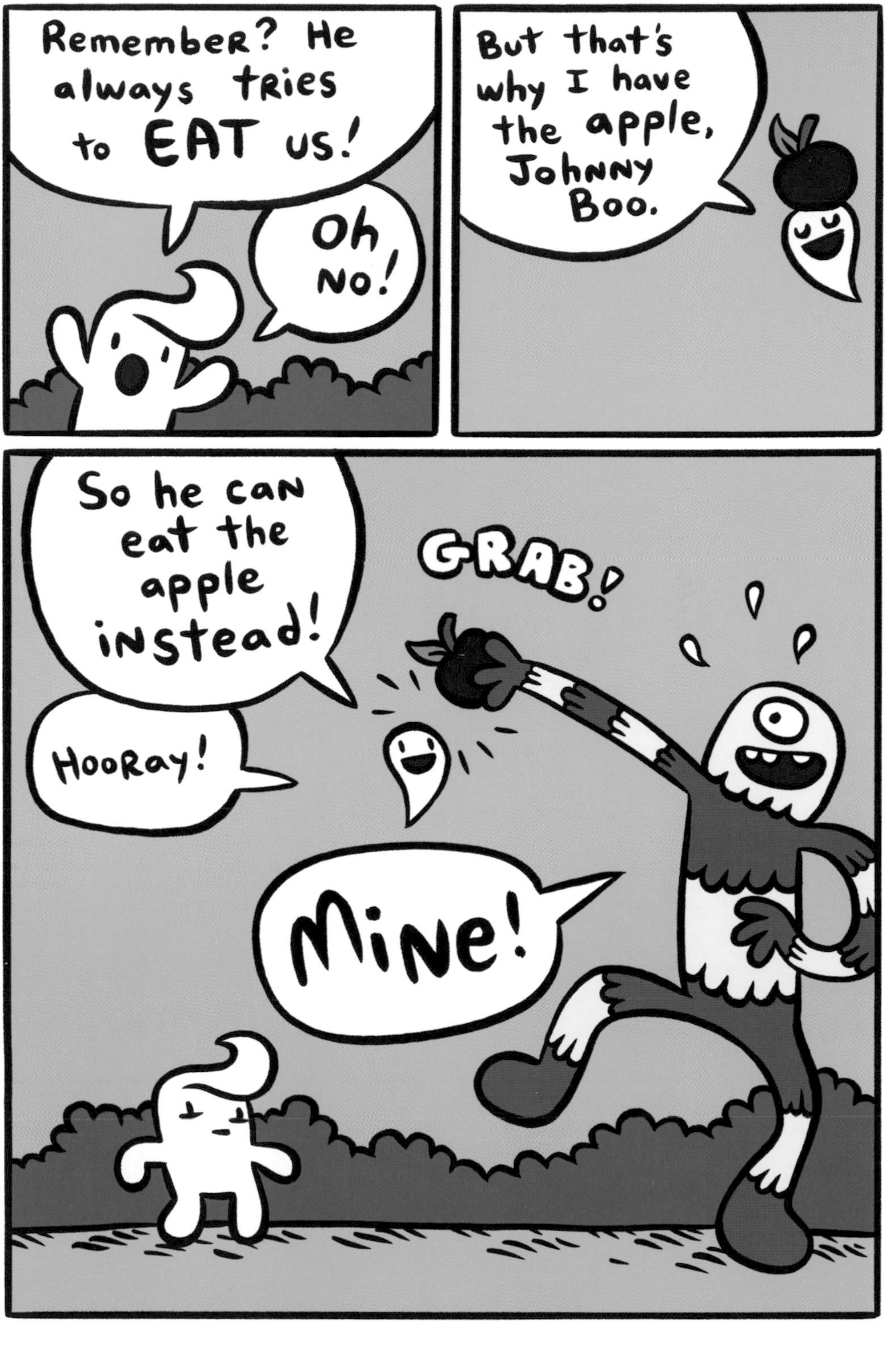
Remember? He always tries to EAT us!
Oh No!
But that's why I have the apple, Johnny Boo.
So he can eat the apple instead!
GRAB!
HooRay!
Mine!

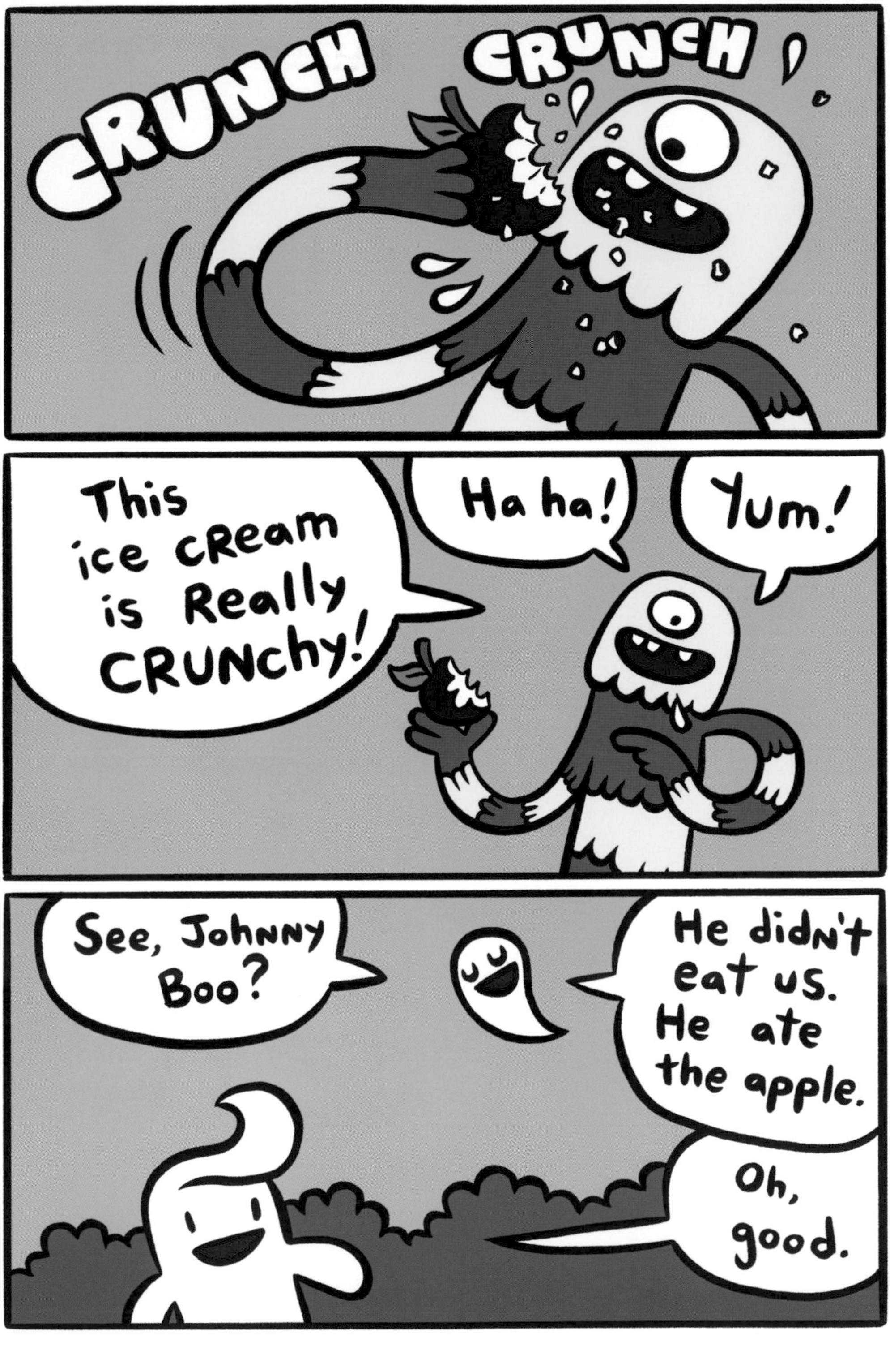
CRUNCH
CRUNCH!
This ice cream is Really CRUNchy!
Ha ha!
Yum!
See, Johnny Boo?
He didn't eat us. He ate the apple.
Oh, good.

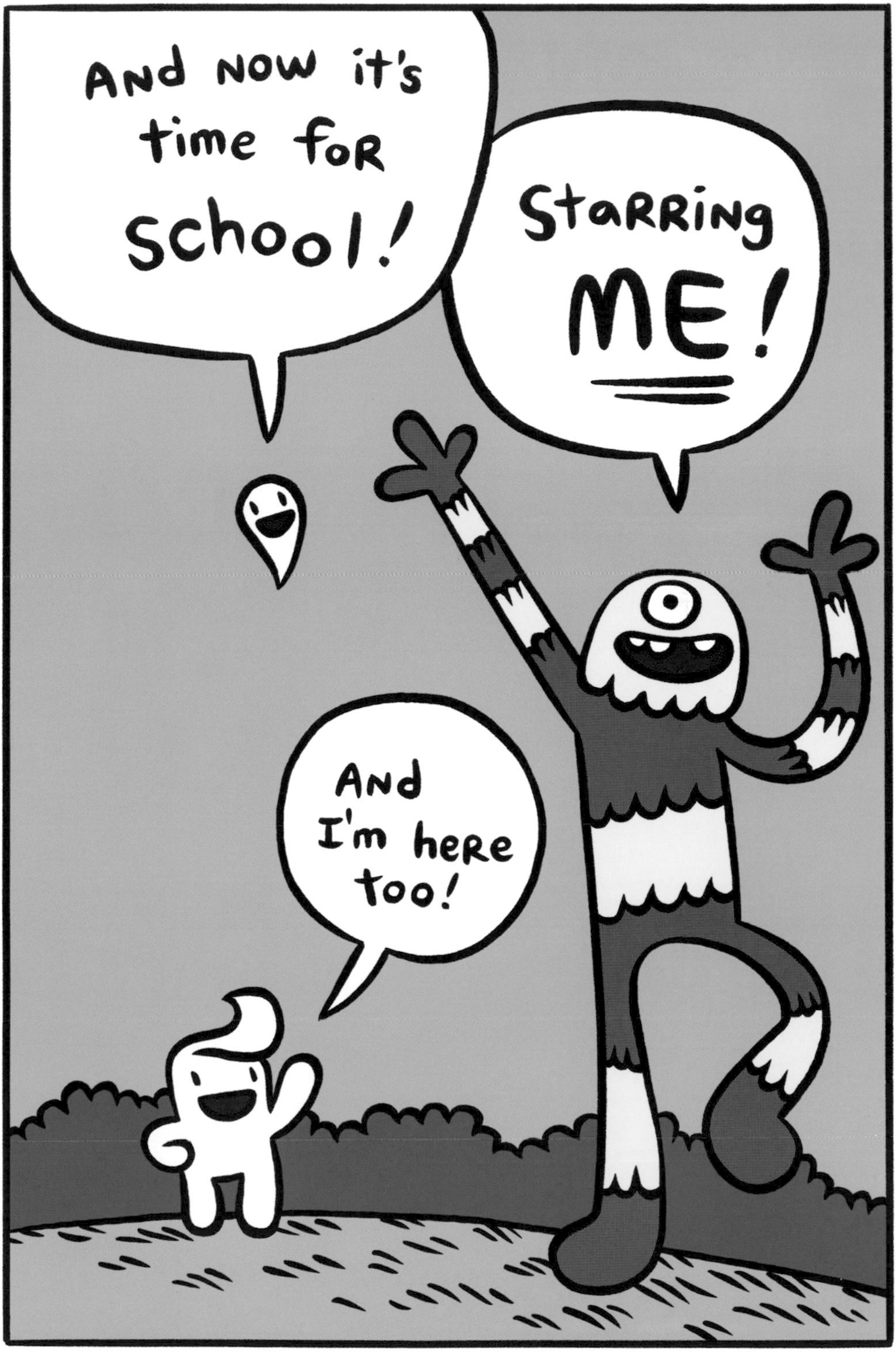
And now it's time for school!
Starring ME!
And I'm here too!

CHAPTER THREE

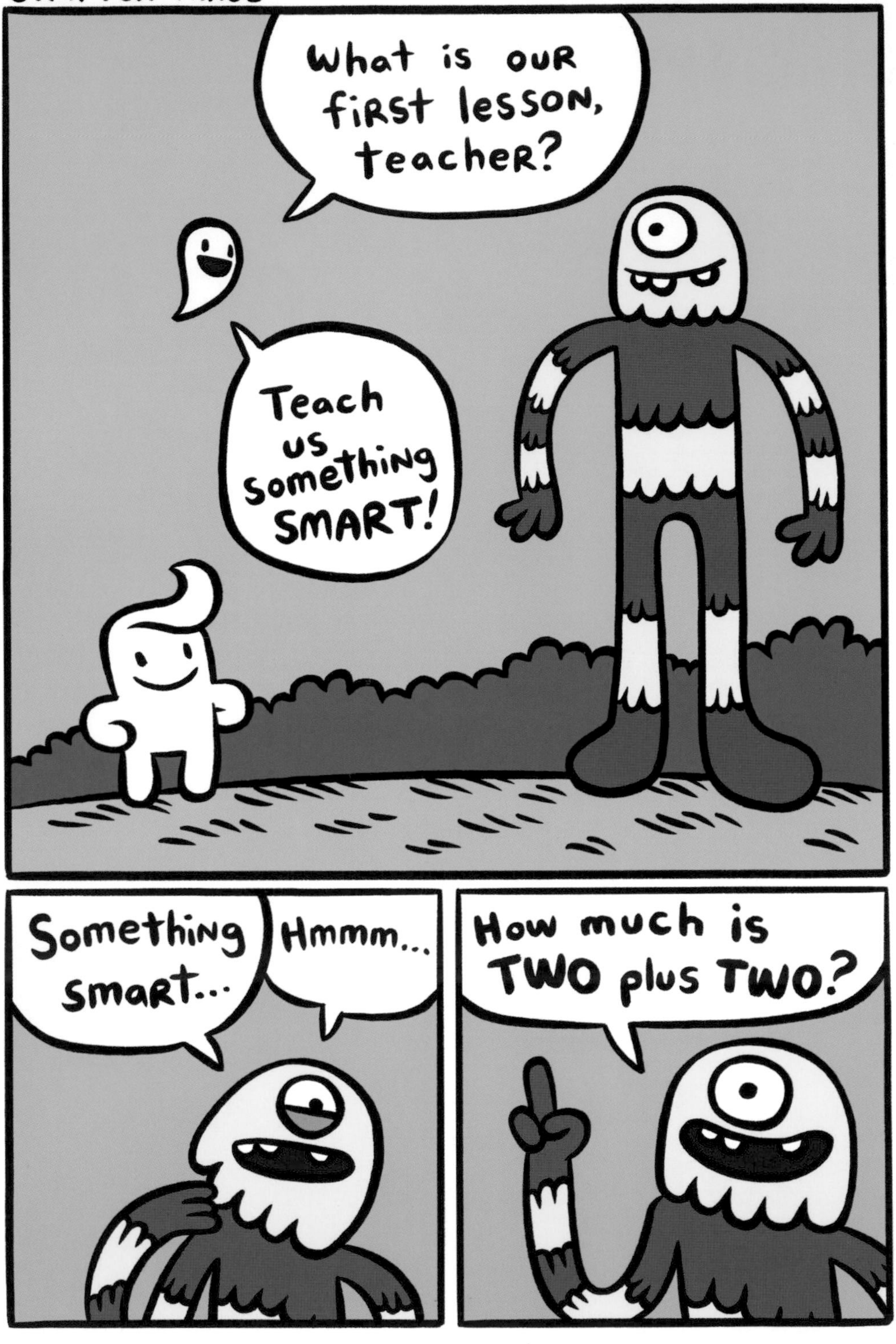
What is our first lesson, teacher?
Teach us something SMART!
Something smart...
Hmmm...
How much is TWO plus TWO?

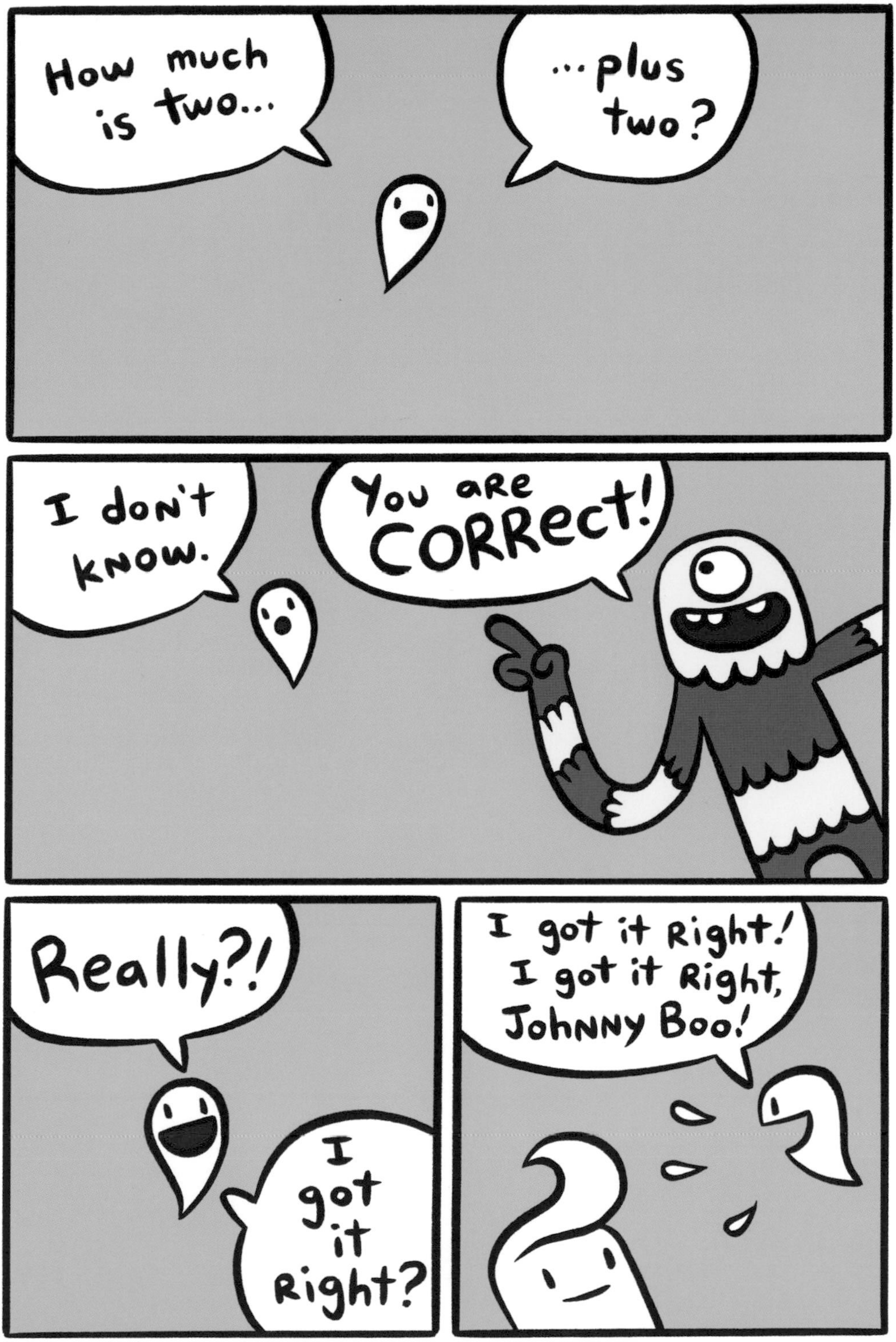
How much is two...
...plus two?
I don't know.
You are CORRECT!
Really?!
I got it right?
I got it right! I got it right, Johnny Boo!

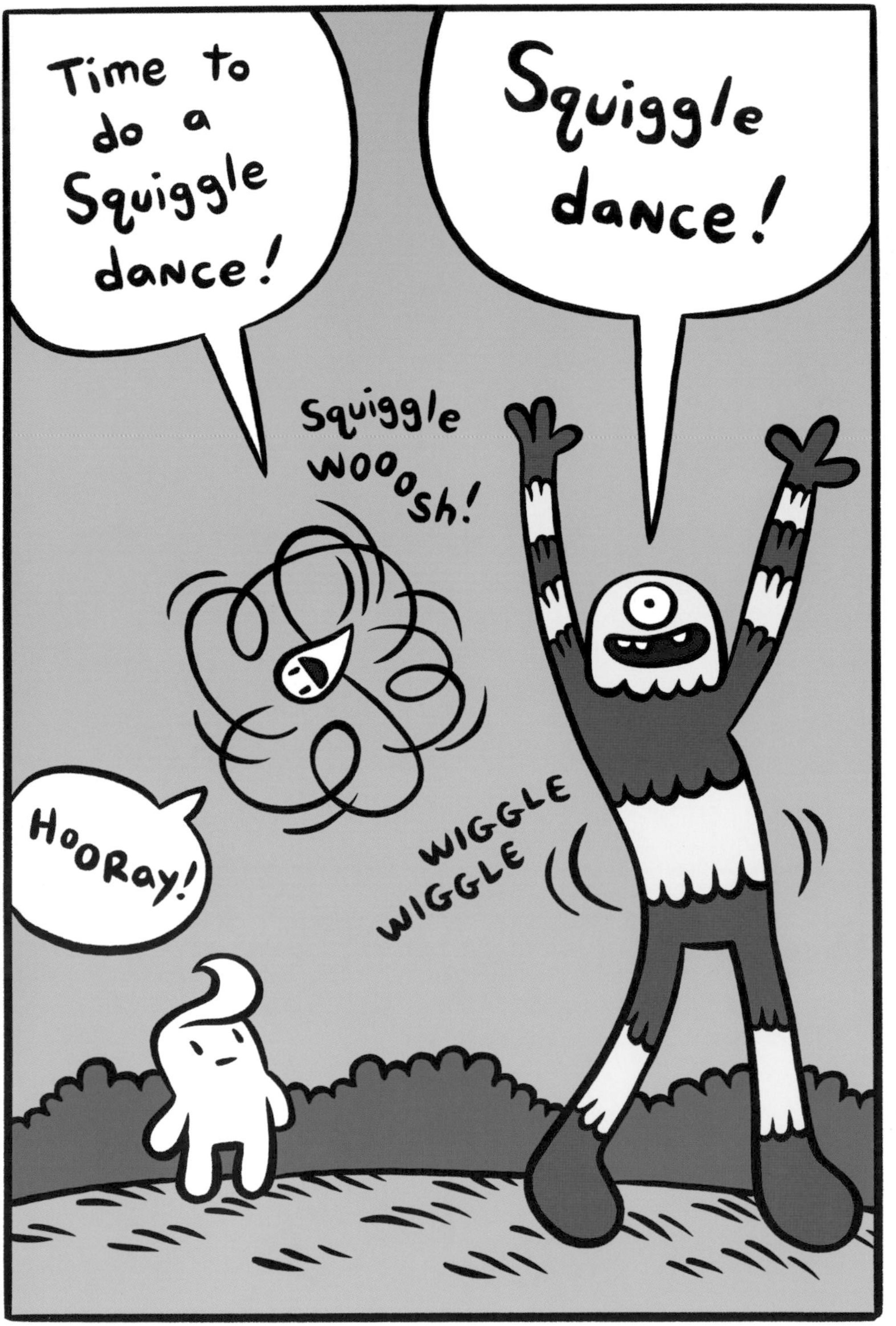
Time to do a Squiggle dance!
Squiggle dance!
Squiggle WOOOOSH!
HOORay!
WIGGLE WIGGLE

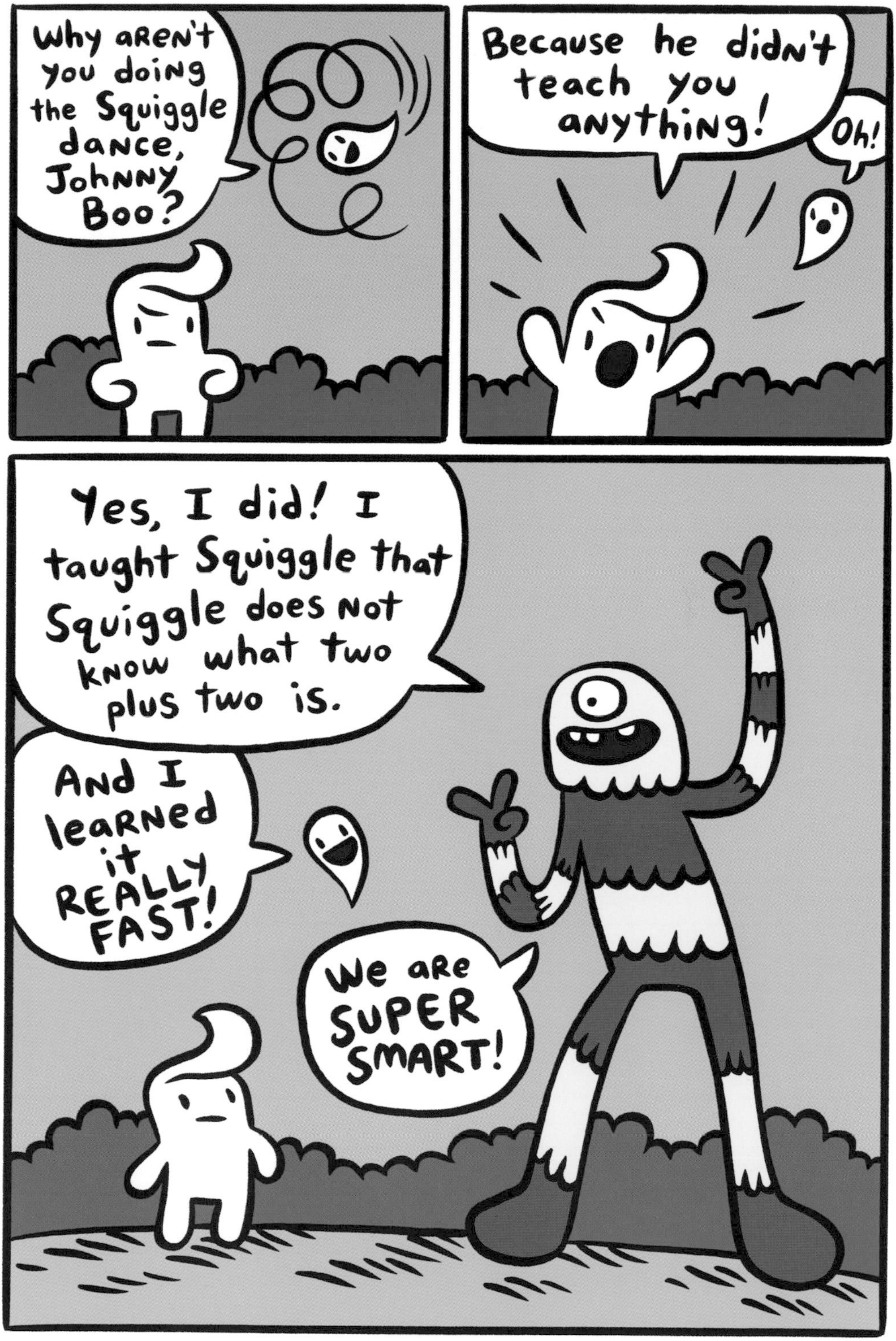
Why aren't you doing the Squiggle dance, Johnny Boo?
Because he didn't teach you anything!
Oh!
Yes, I did! I taught Squiggle that Squiggle does not know what two plus two is.
And I learned it REALLY FAST!
We are SUPER SMART!

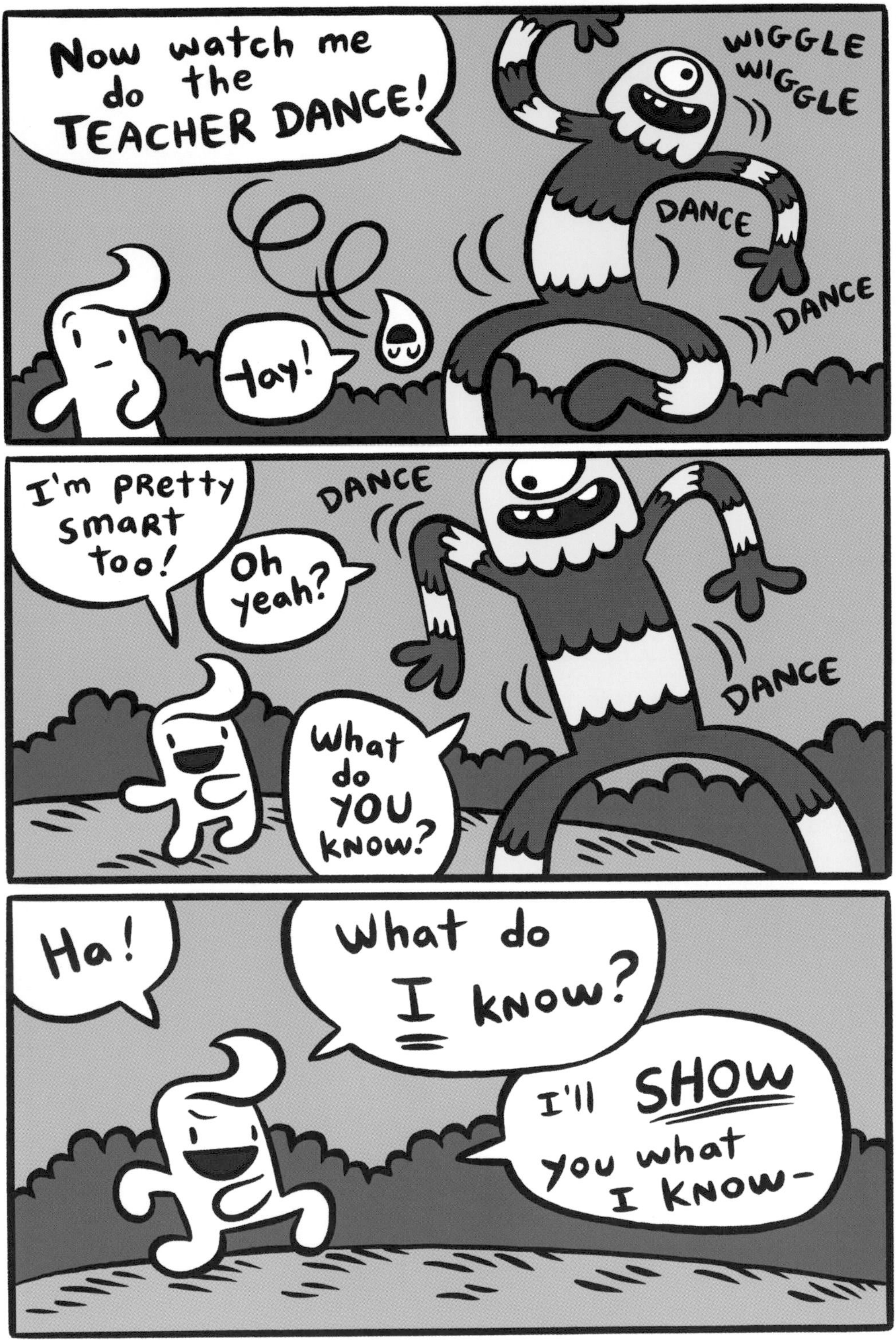

Now watch me do the TEACHER DANCE!
WIGGLE WIGGLE
DANCE
DANCE
-tay!
I'm pretty smart too!
Oh yeah?
DANCE
DANCE
What do YOU know?
Ha!
What do I know?
I'll SHOW you what I know-

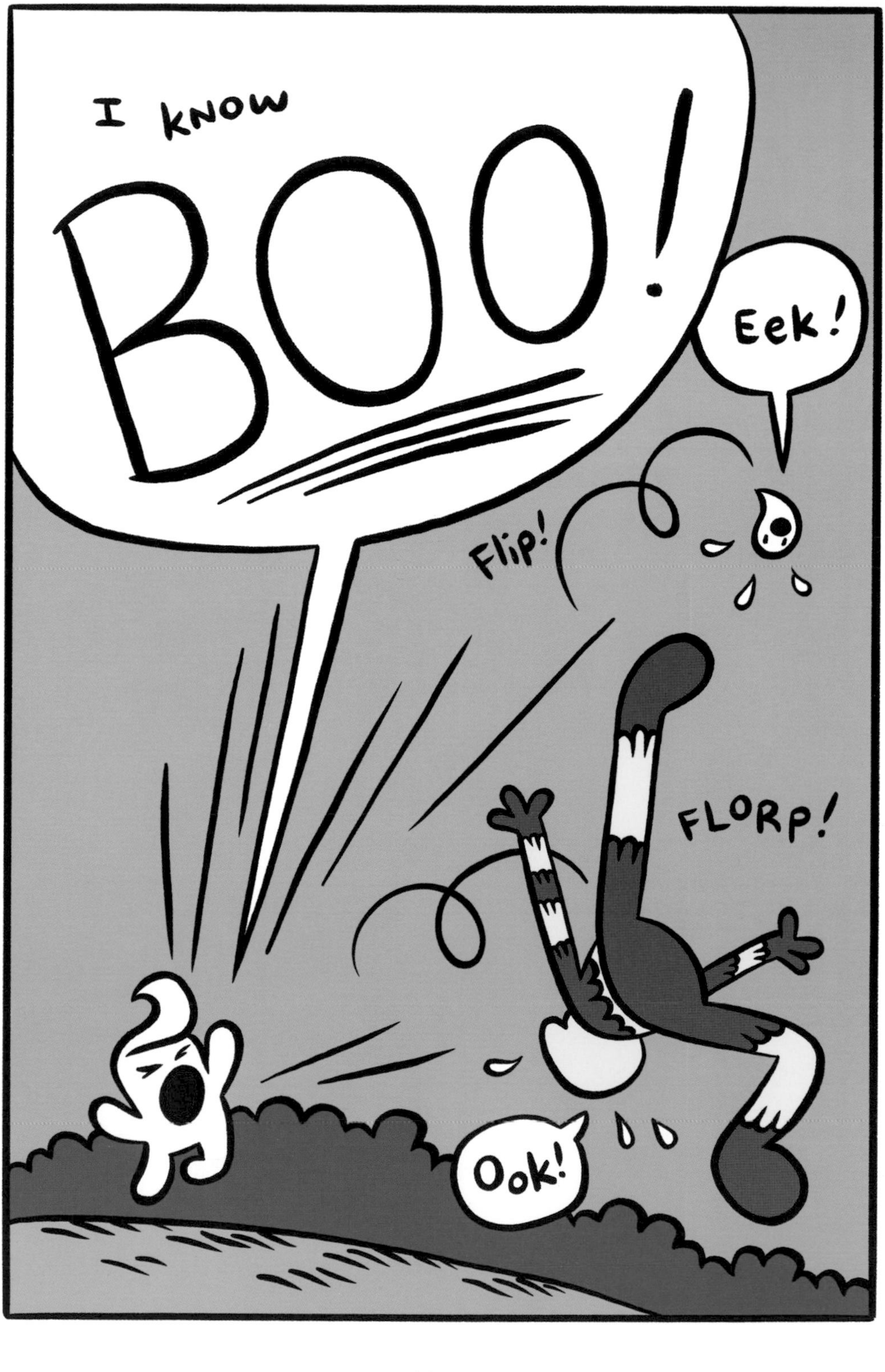
I KNOW
BOO!
Eek!
Flip!
FLORP!
Ook!

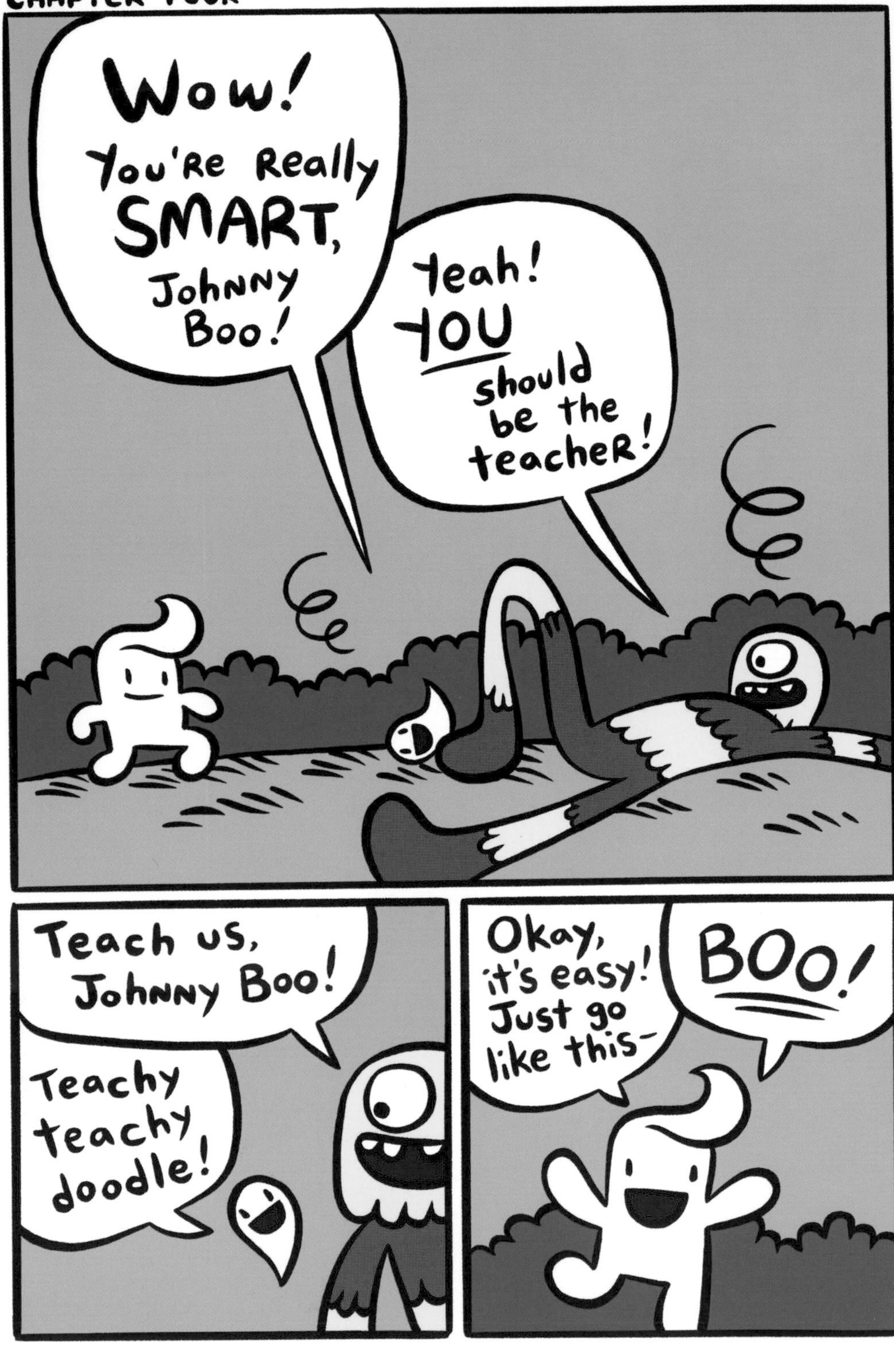
Wow! You're Really SMART, Johnny Boo!
Yeah! YOU should be the teacher!
Teach us, Johnny Boo!
Teachy teachy doodle!
Okay, it's easy! Just go like this-
BOO!

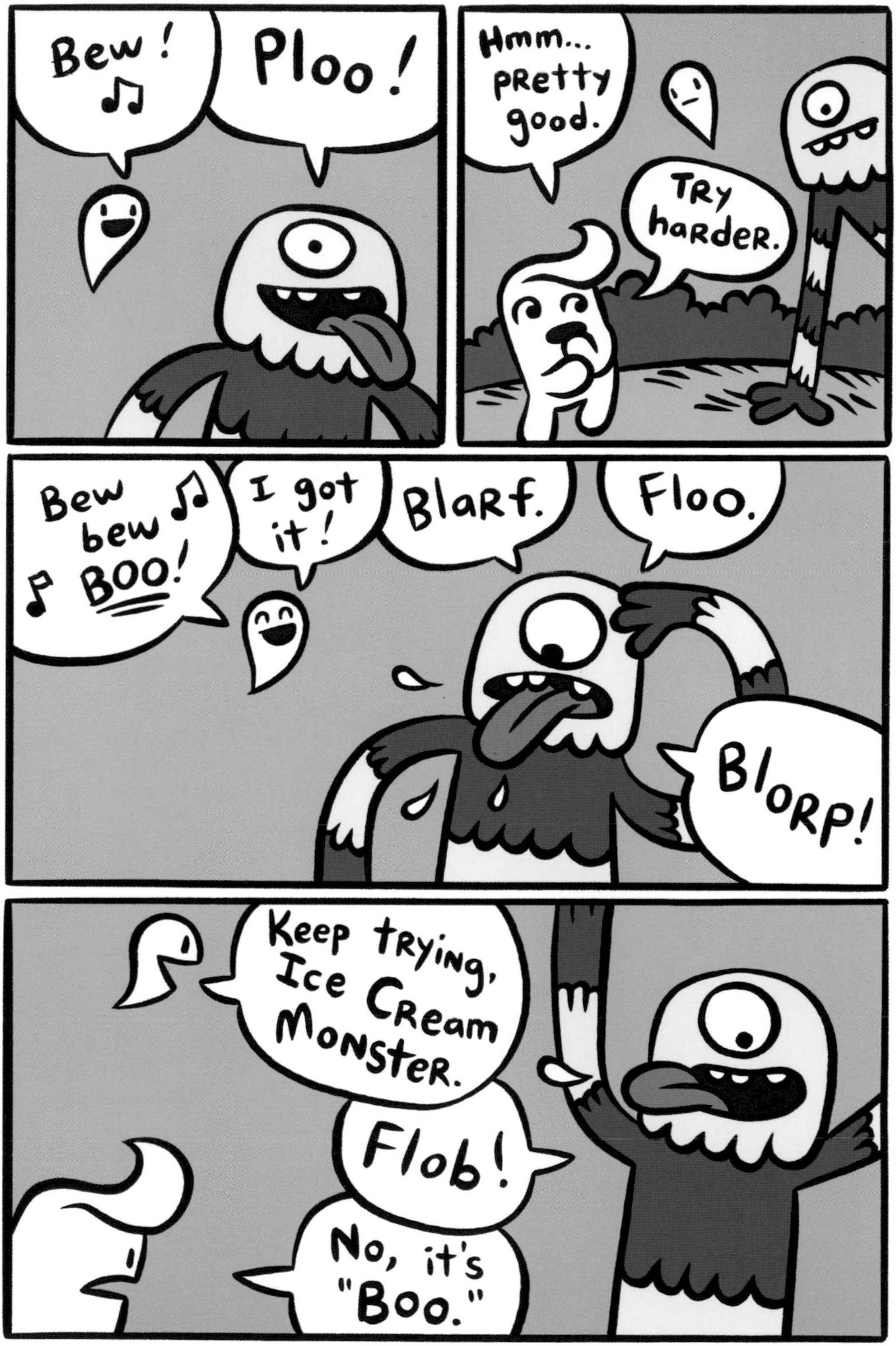
Bew! ♫
Ploo!
Hmm... pretty good.
Try harder.
Bew bew ♫ ♪ BOO!
I got it!
Blarf.
Floo.
Blorp!
Keep trying, Ice Cream Monster.
Flob!
No, it's "Boo."

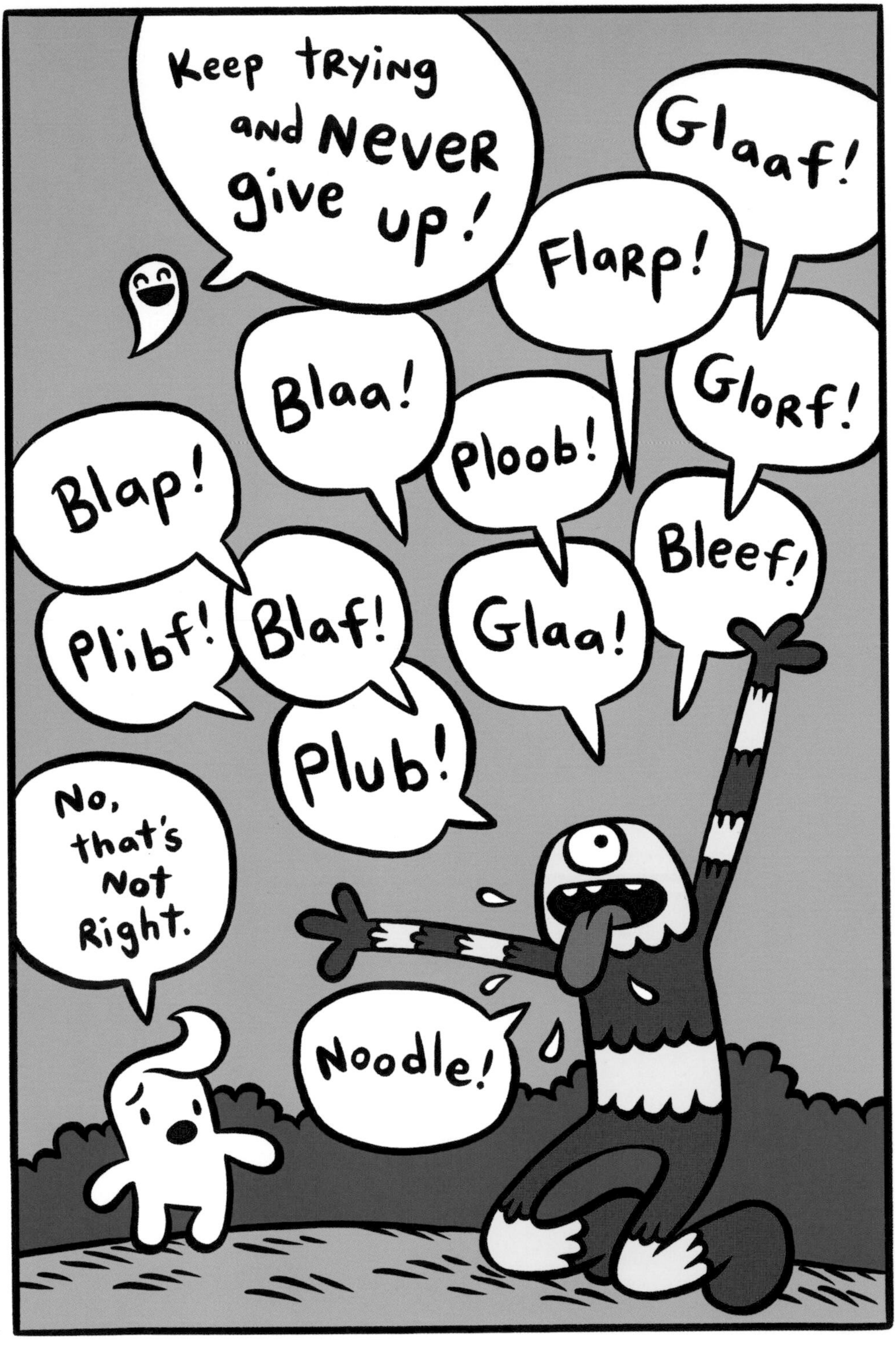
Keep trying and Never give up!
Glaaf!
Flarp!
Blaa!
Glorf!
Ploob!
Blap!
Bleef!
Plibf!
Blaf!
Glaa!
Plub!
No, that's Not Right.
Noodle!

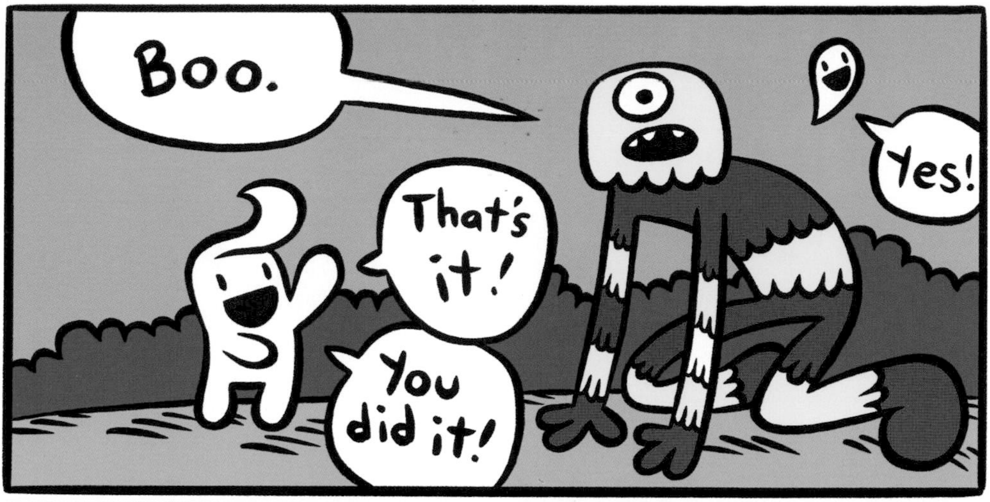
Boo.
That's it!
You did it!
Yes!

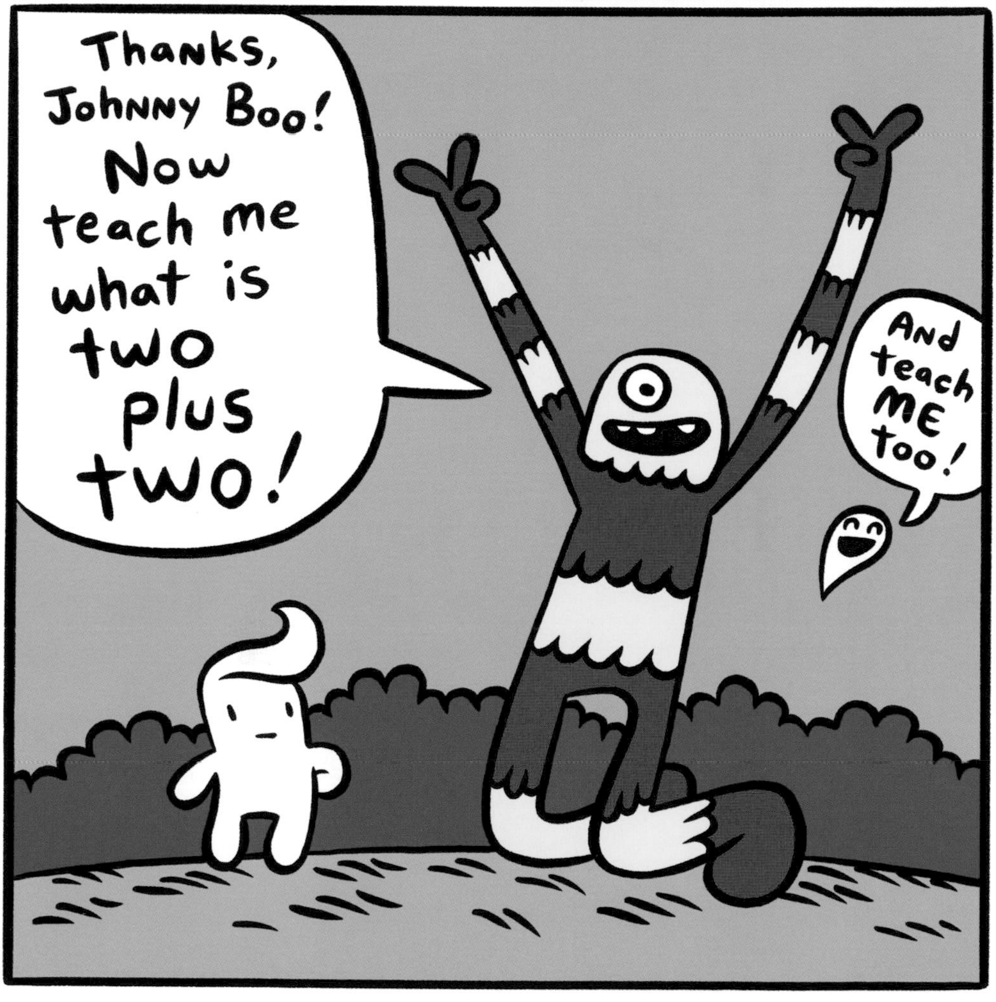
Thanks, Johnny Boo! Now teach me what is two plus two!
And teach ME too!

CHAPTER FIVE

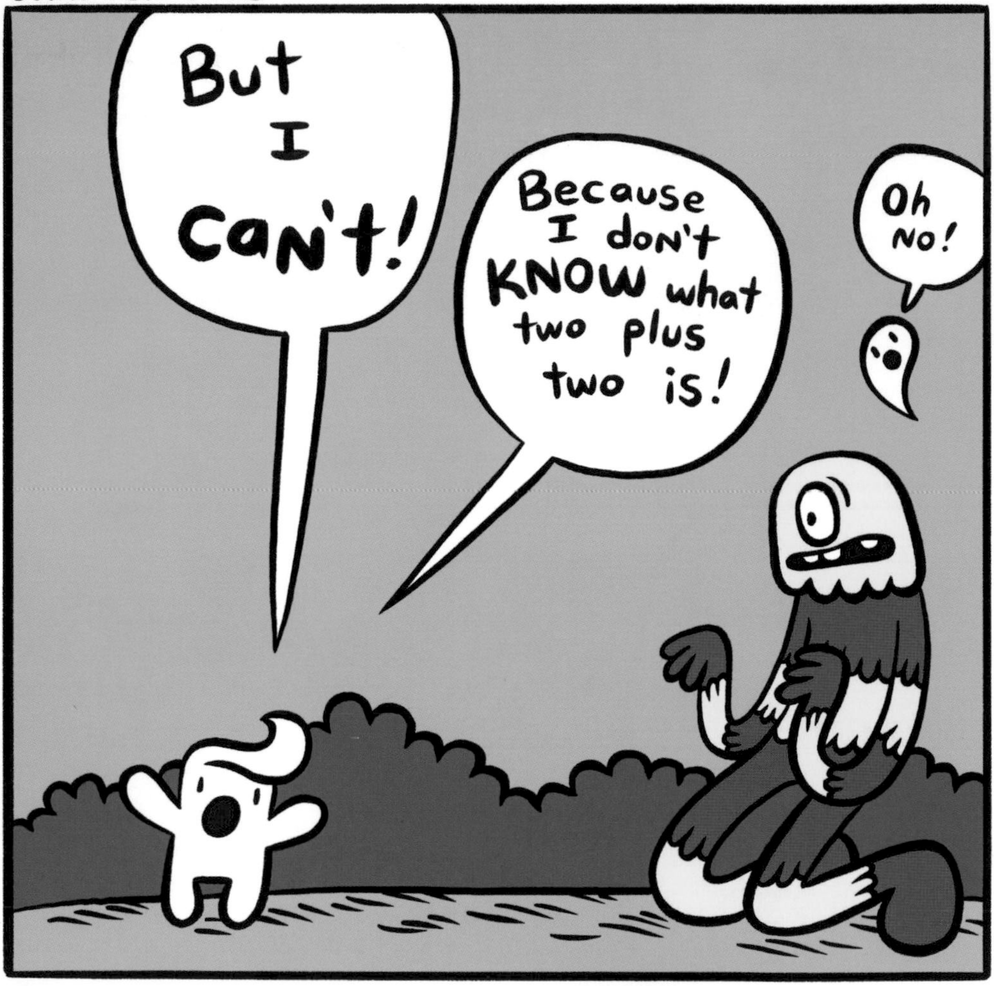
But I can't!
Because I don't KNOW what two plus two is!
Oh No!

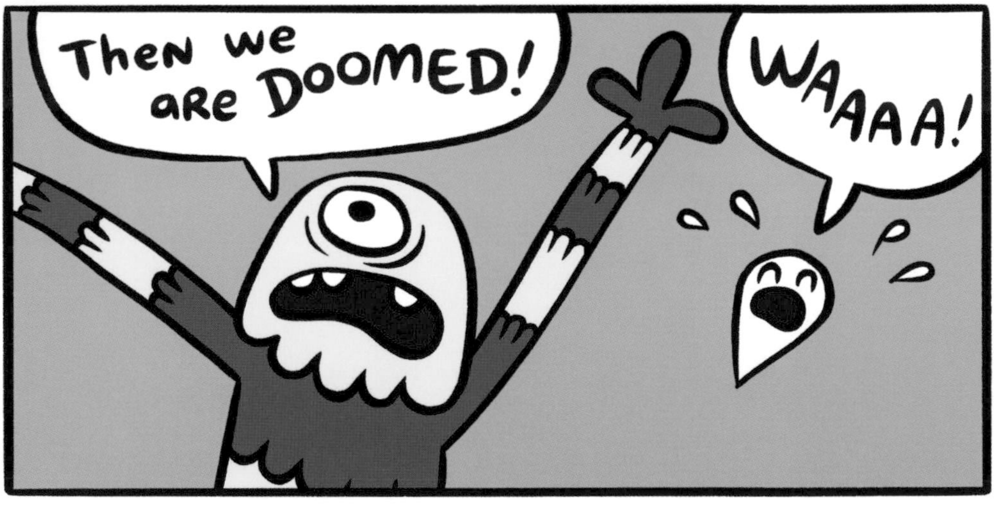
Then we are DOOMED!
WAAAAA!

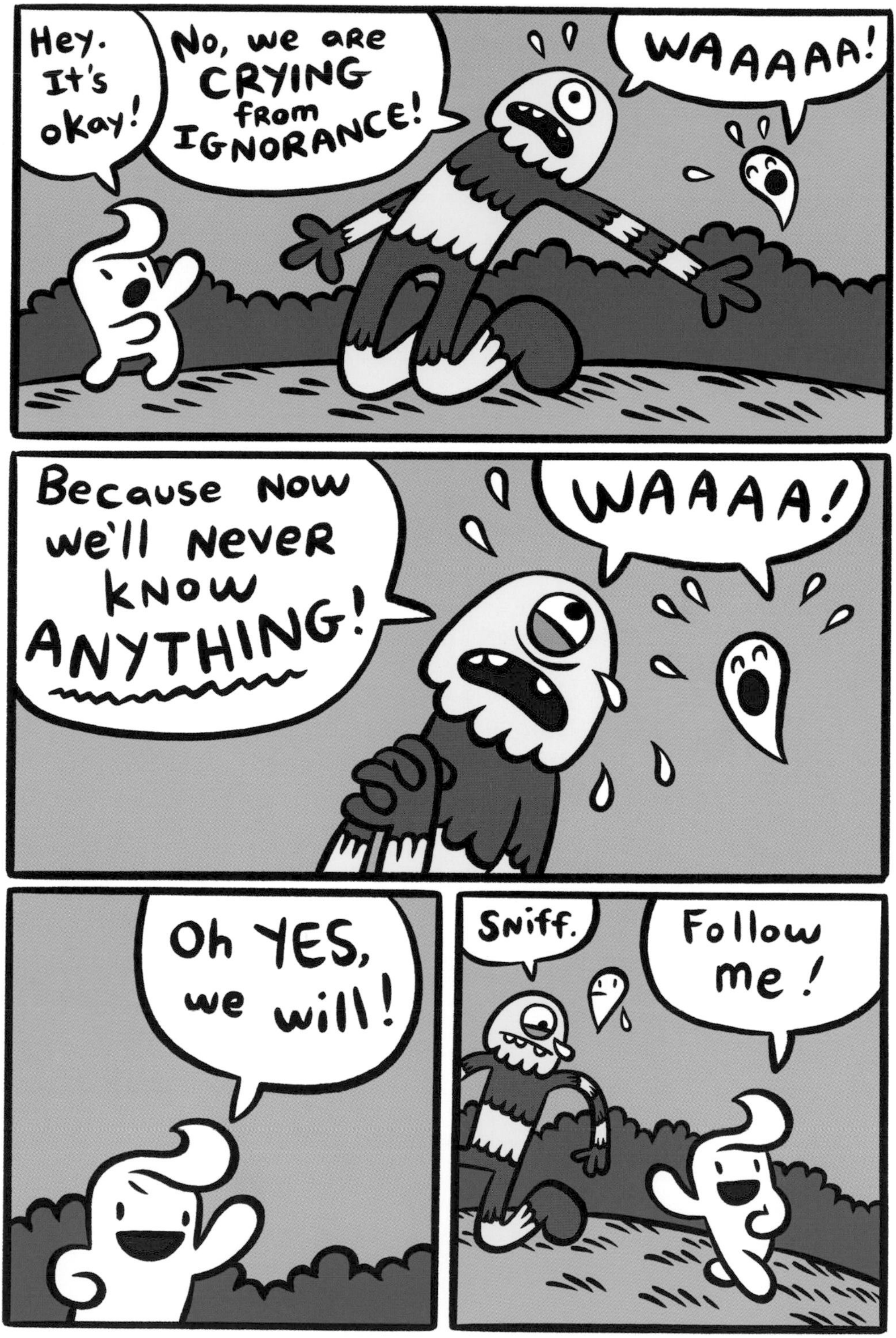

Hey. It's okay!
No, we are CRYING from IGNORANCE!
WAAAAA!
Because now we'll never know ANYTHING!
WAAAA!
Oh YES, we will!
Sniff.
Follow me!

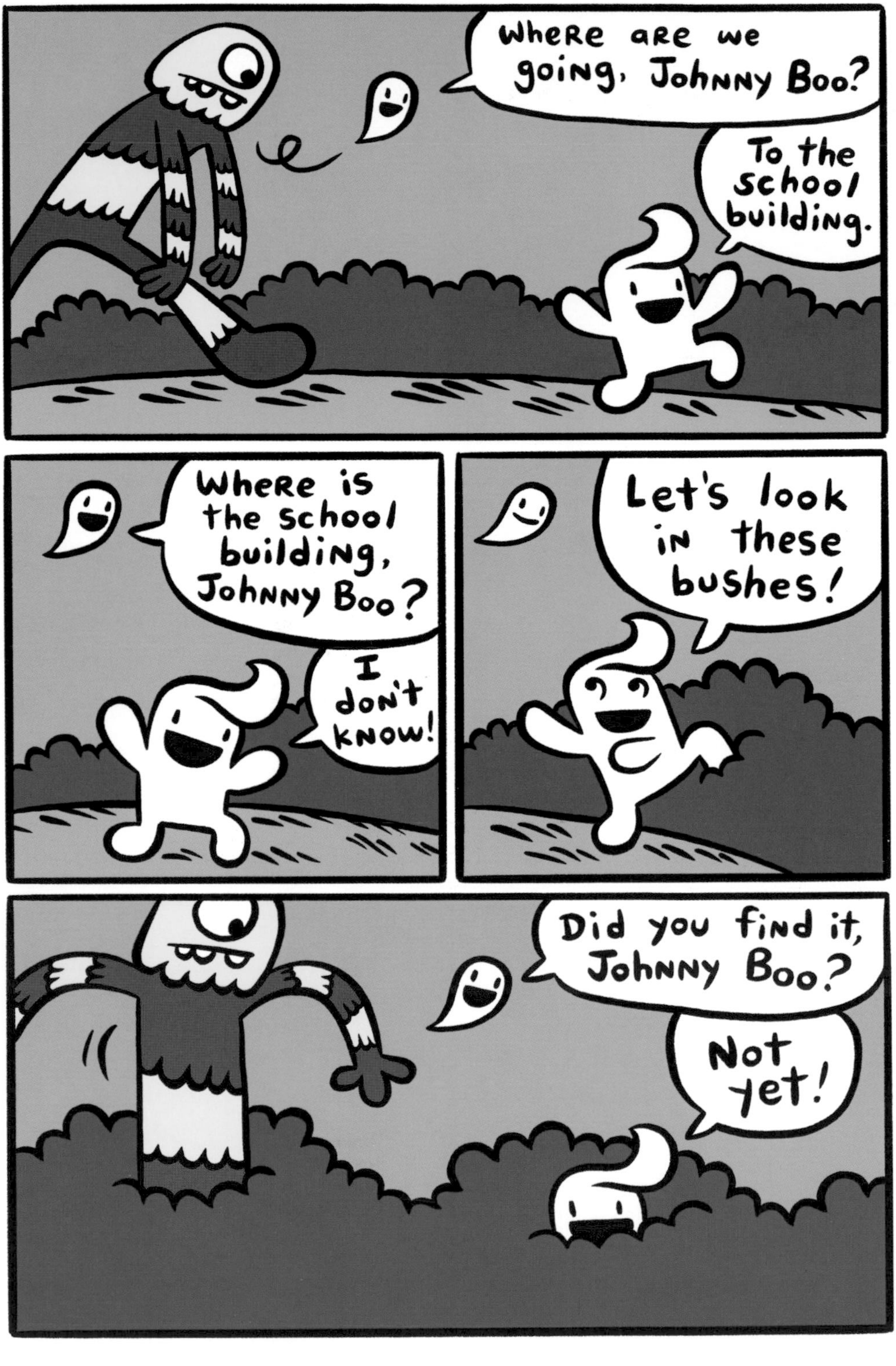
Where are we going, Johnny Boo?
To the school building.
Where is the school building, Johnny Boo?
I don't know!
Let's look in these bushes!
Did you find it, Johnny Boo?
Not yet!

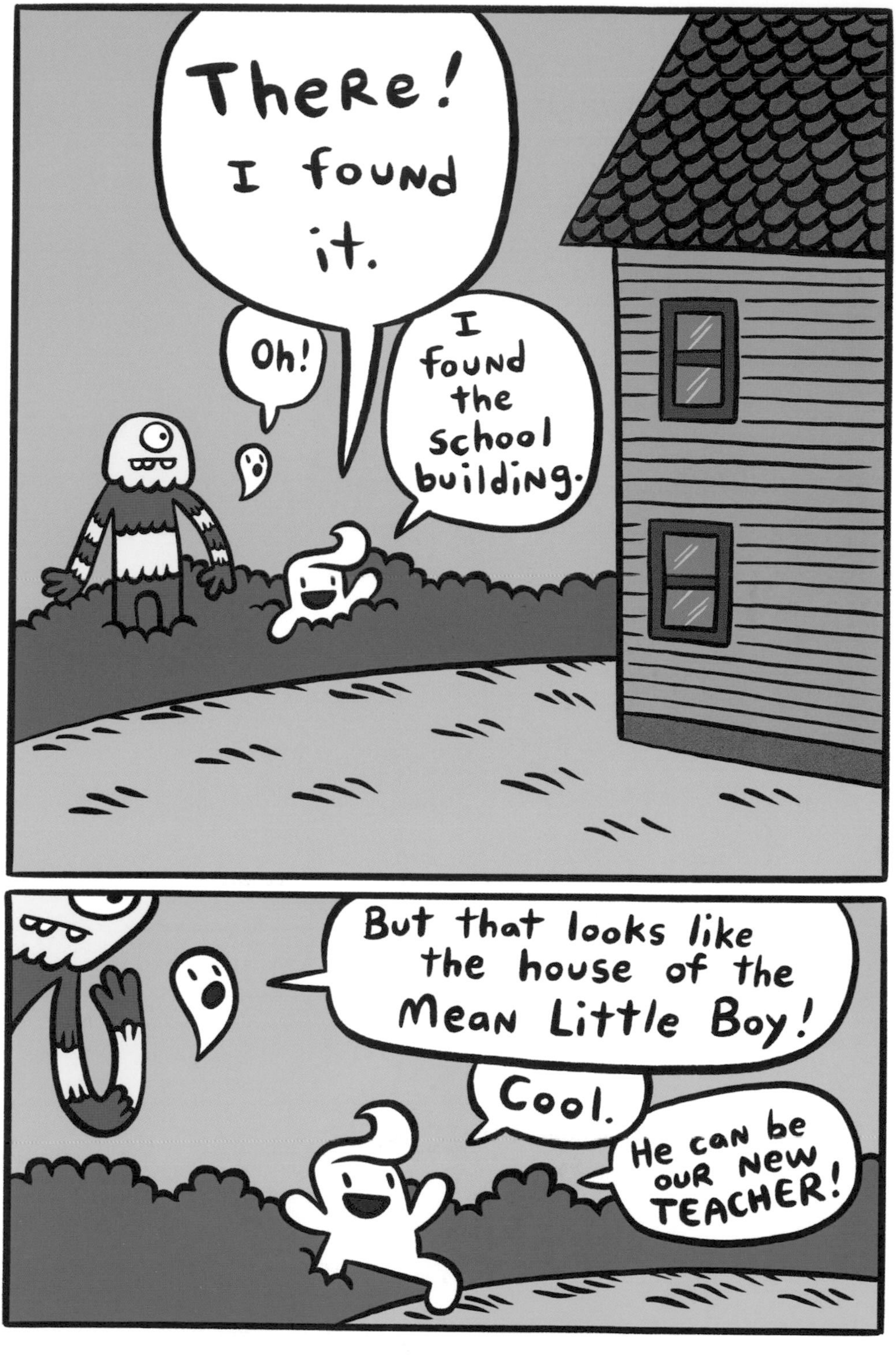
There! I found it.
Oh!
I found the school building.
But that looks like the house of the Mean Little Boy!
Cool.
He can be our NEW TEACHER!

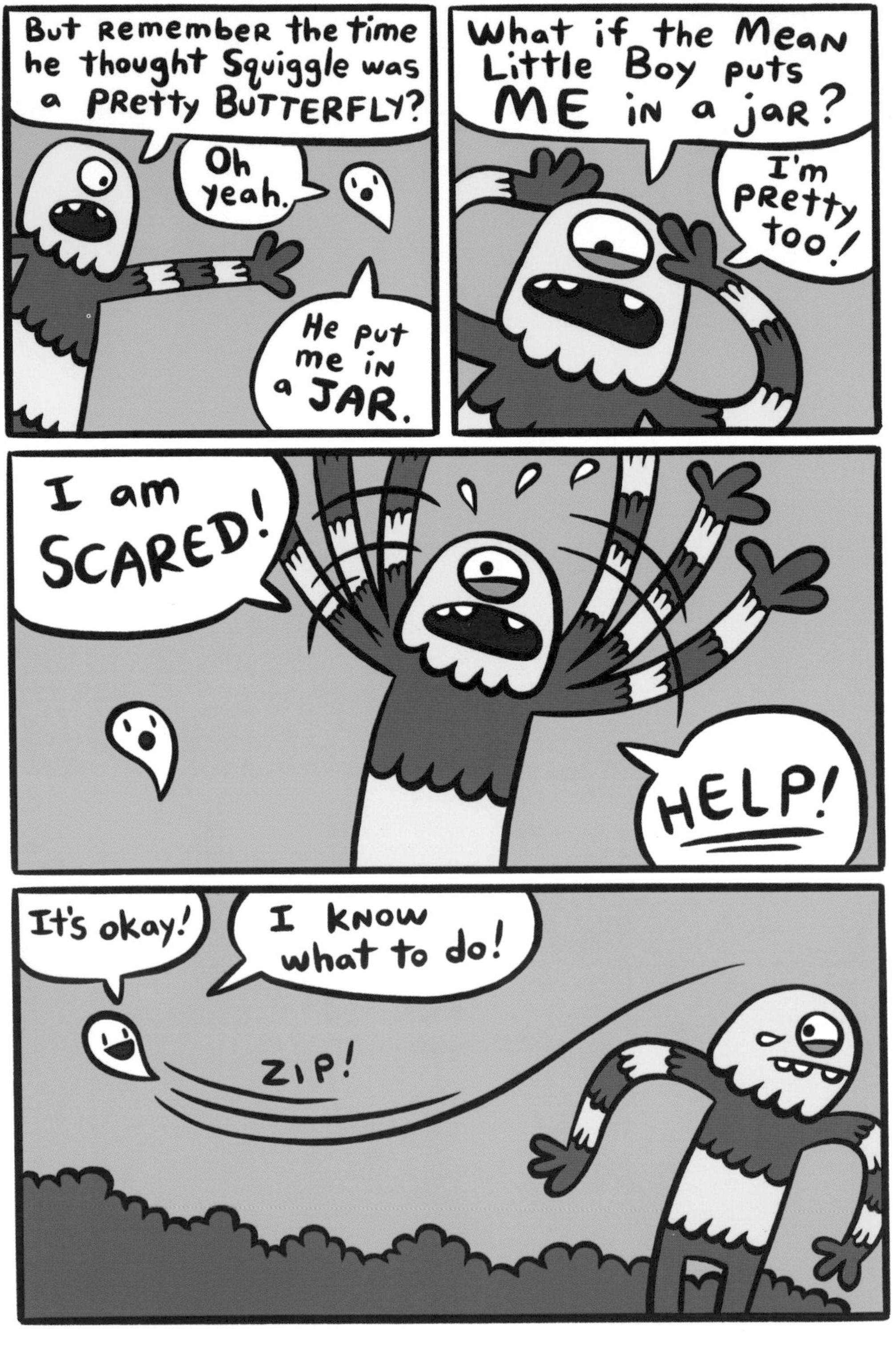
But remember the time he thought Squiggle was a PRETTY BUTTERFLY?
Oh yeah.
He put me in a JAR.
What if the Mean Little Boy puts ME in a jar?
I'm pretty too!
I am SCARED!
HELP!
It's okay!
I know what to do!
ZIP!

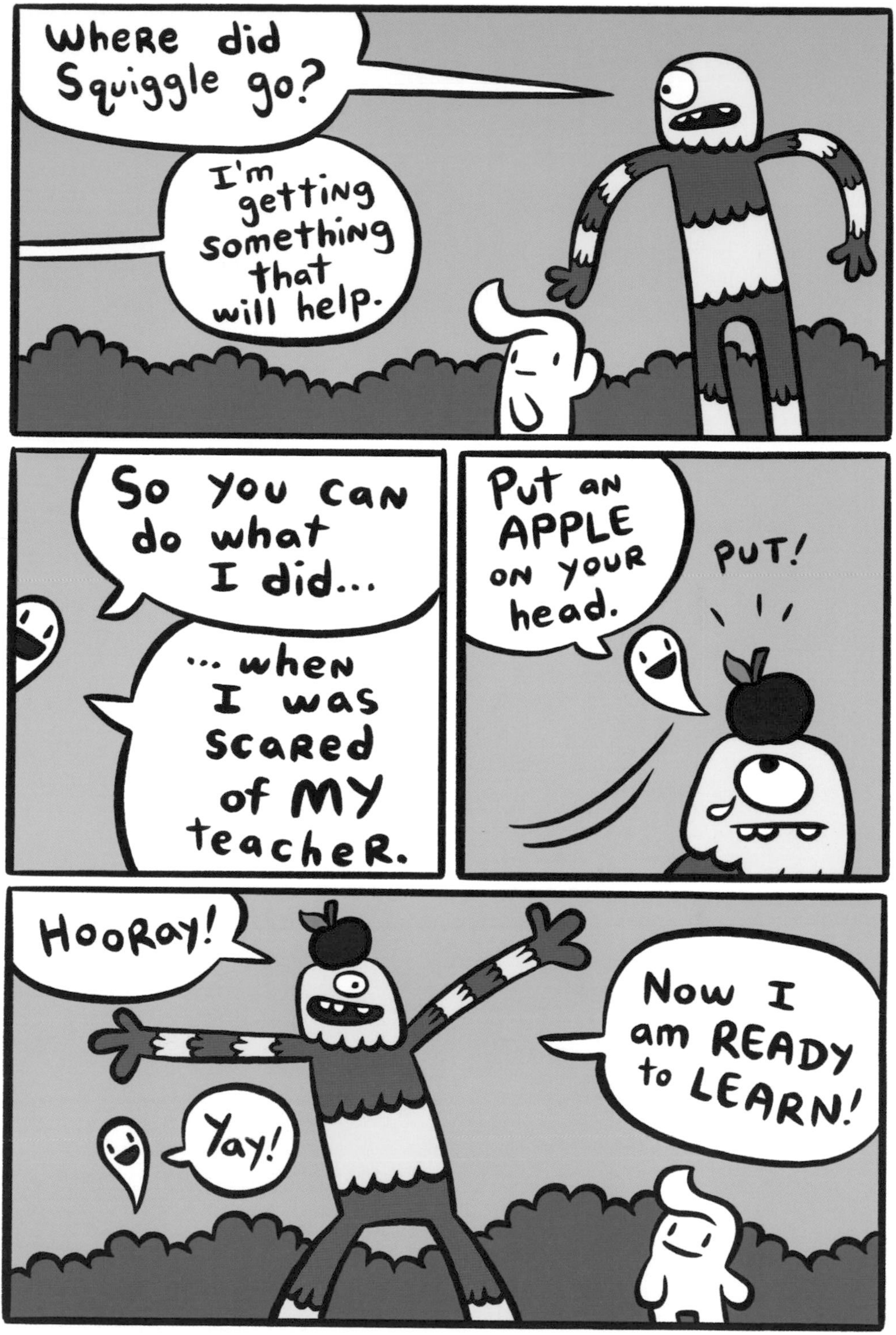
Where did Squiggle go?
I'm getting something that will help.
So you can do what I did...
...when I was scared of MY teacher.
Put an APPLE on your head.
PUT!
HOORAY!
Now I am READY to LEARN!
Yay!

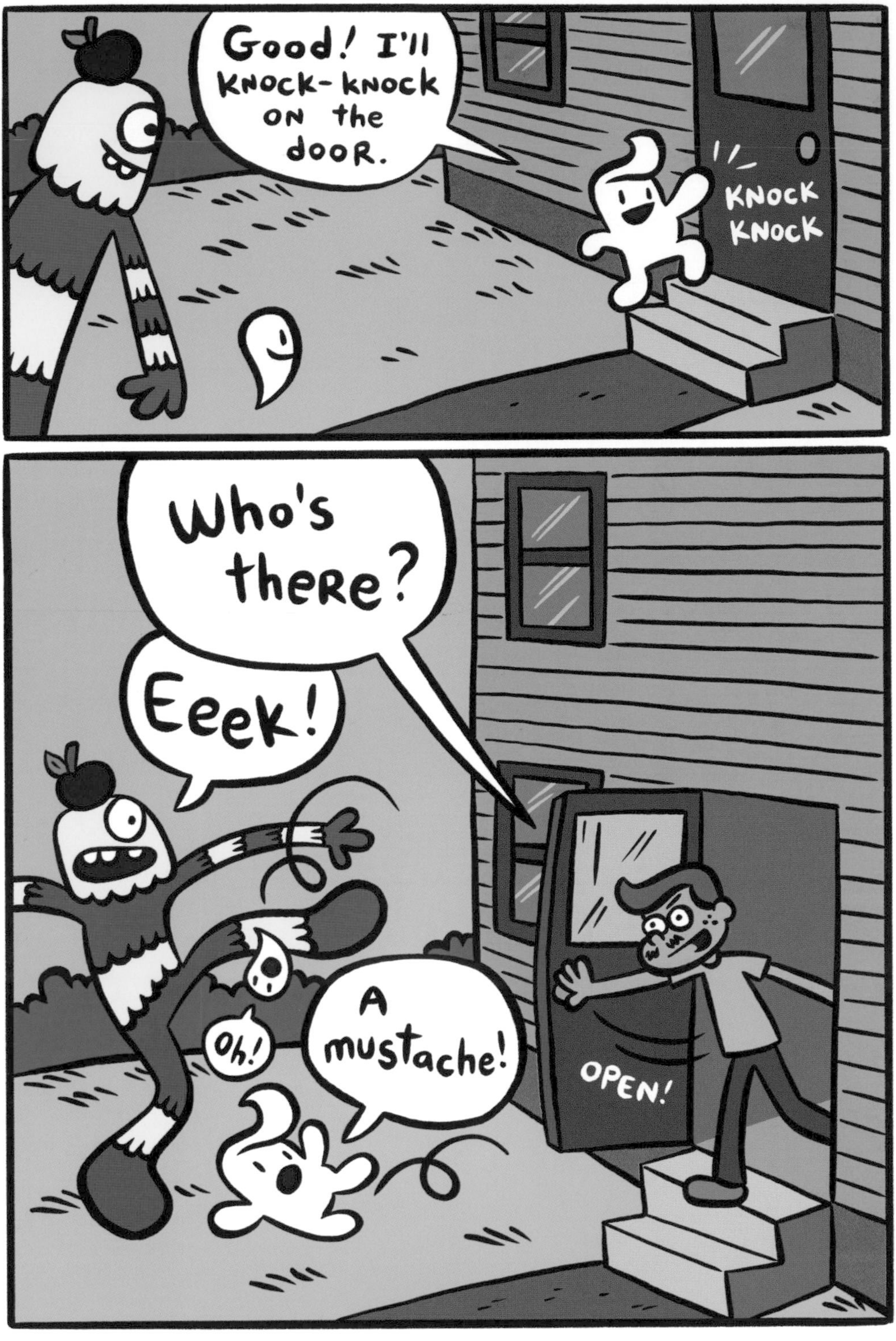
Good! I'll knock-knock on the door.
KNOCK KNOCK
Who's there?
Eeek!
Oh!
A mustache!
OPEN!

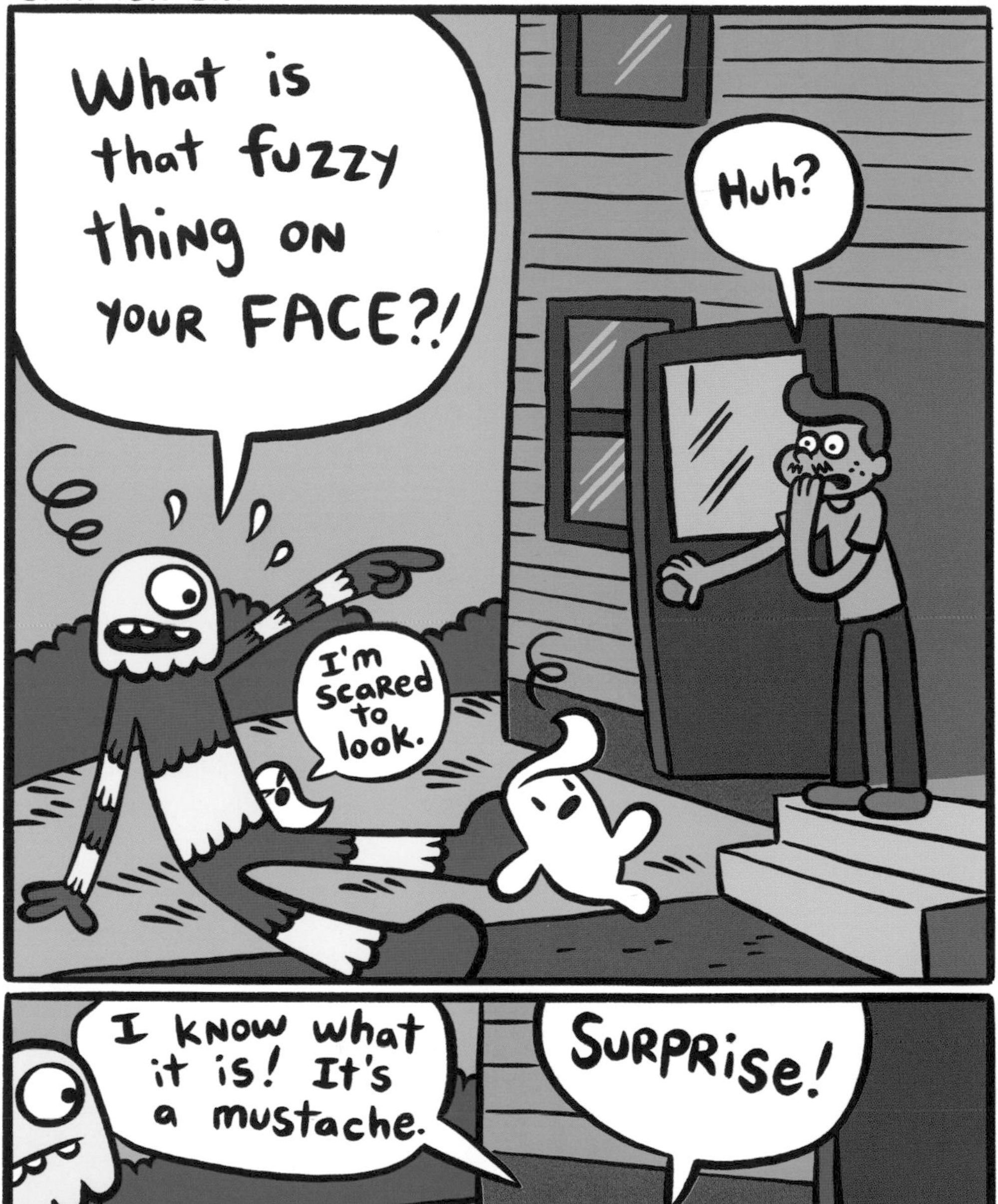
What is that fuzzy thing on your FACE?!
Huh?
I'm scared to look.

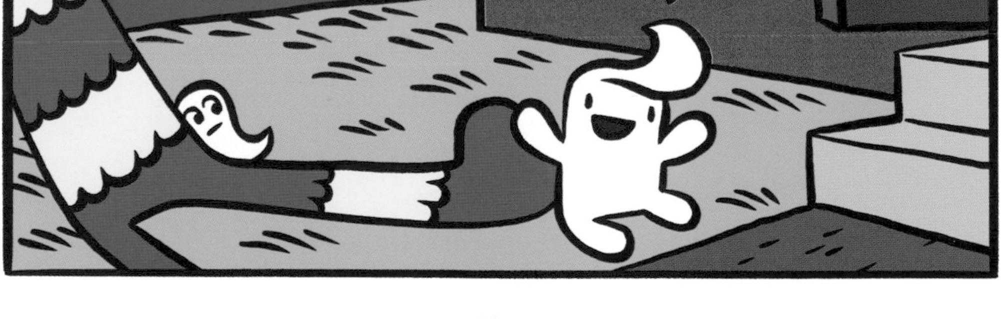
I know what it is! It's a mustache.
SURPRISE!

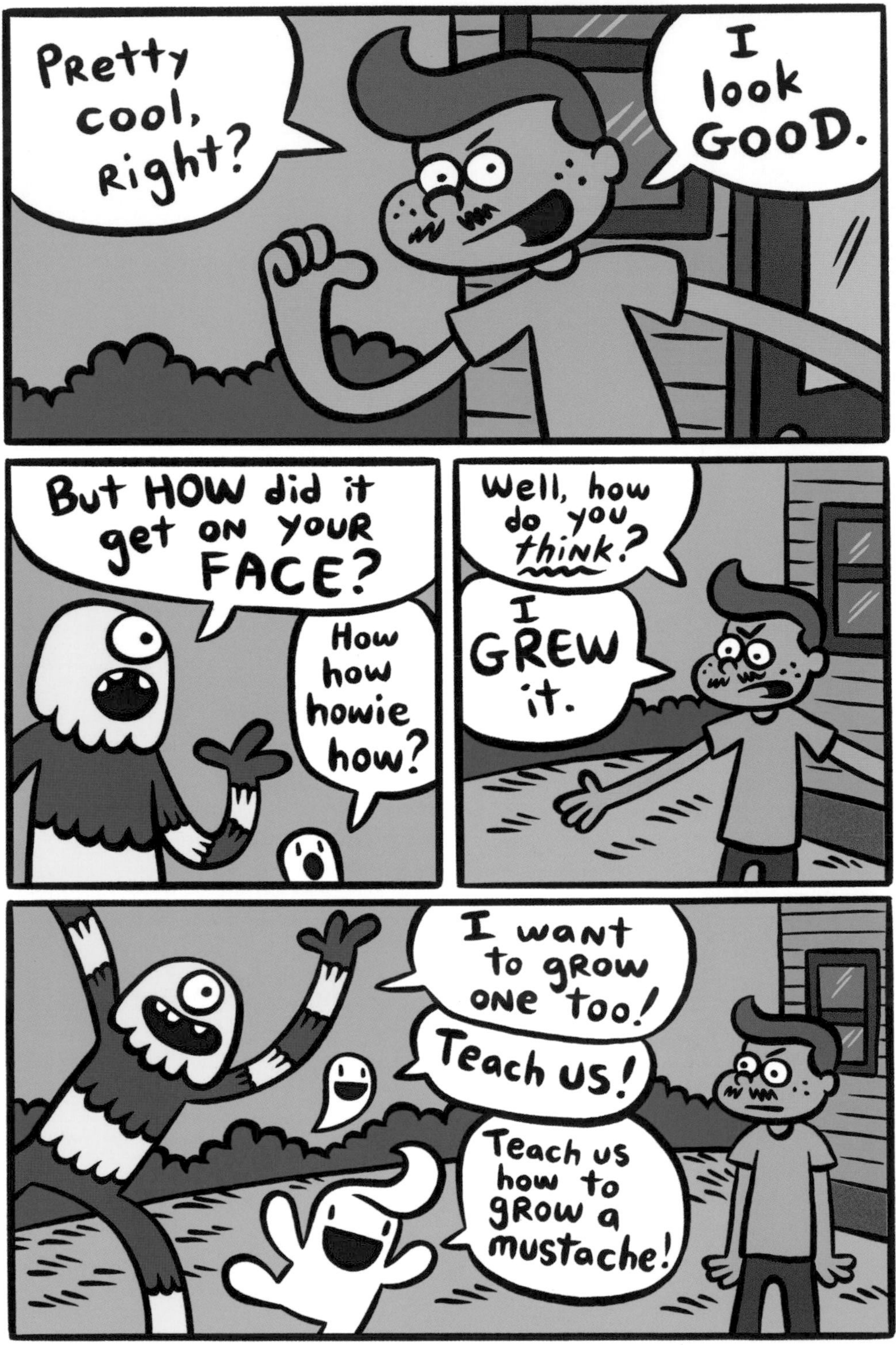
Pretty cool, Right?
I look GOOD.
But HOW did it get on YOUR FACE?
How how howie how?
Well, how do you think?
I GREW it.
I want to grow one too!
Teach us!
Teach us how to grow a mustache!

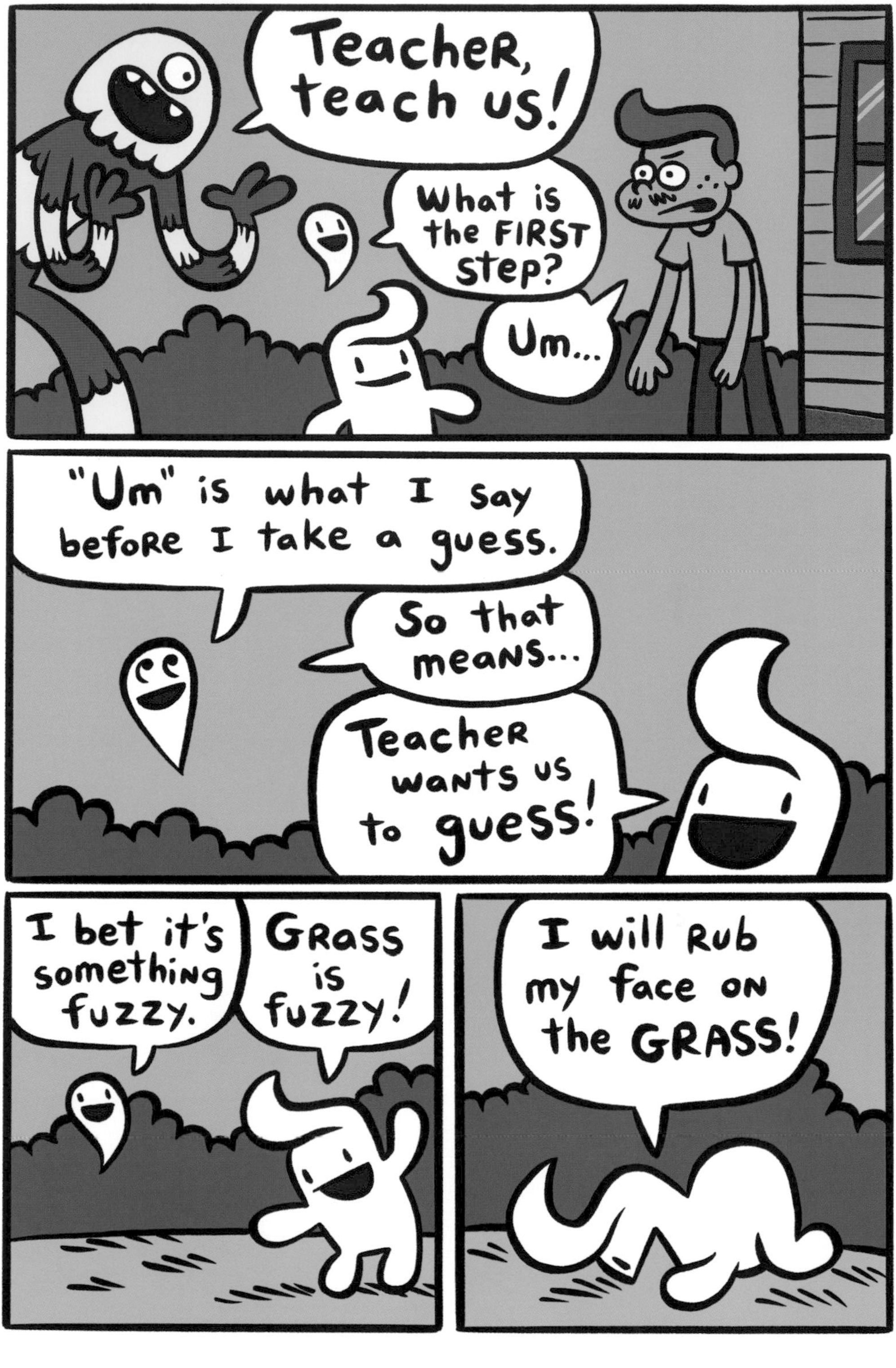
Teacher, teach us!
What is the FIRST step?
Um...
"Um" is what I say before I take a guess.
So that means...
Teacher wants us to guess!
I bet it's something fuzzy.
Grass is fuzzy!
I will rub my face on the GRASS!

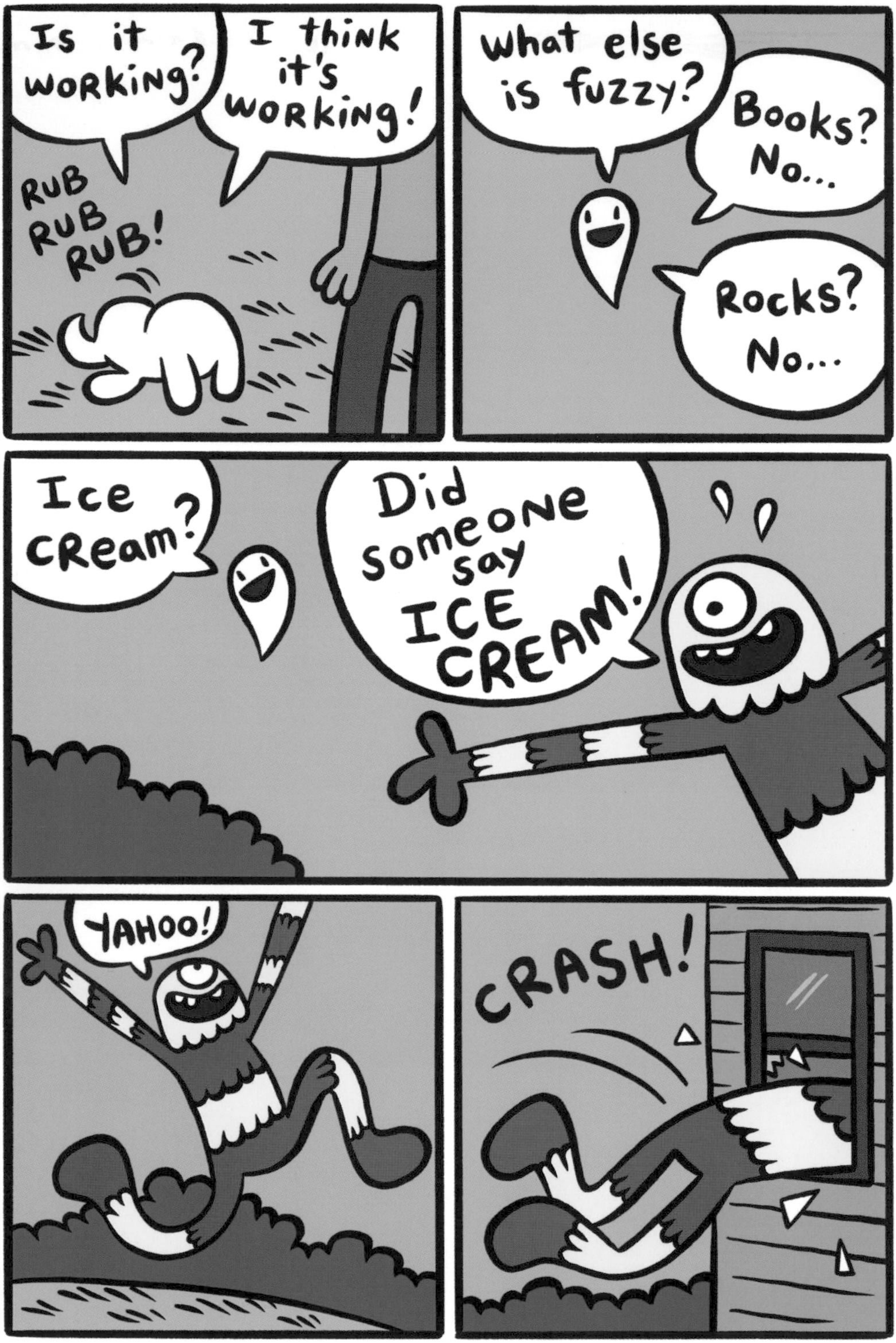

Is it working?
I think it's working!
RUB RUB RUB!
What else is fuzzy?
Books? No...
Rocks? No...
Ice cream?
Did someone say ICE CREAM!
YAHOO!
CRASH!

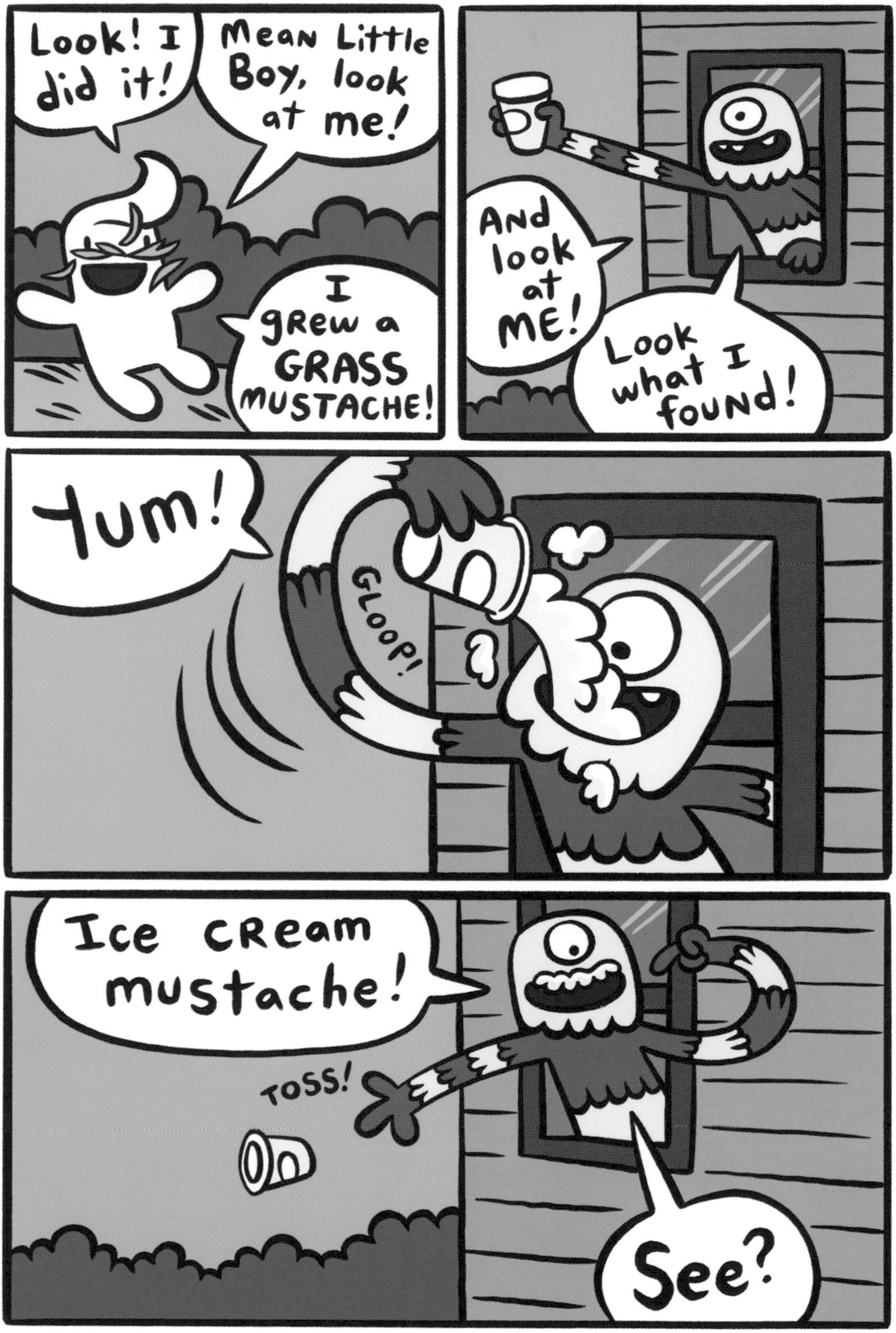
Look! I did it!
Mean Little Boy, look at me!
I grew a GRASS MUSTACHE!
And look at ME!
Look what I found!
Yum!
GLOOP!
Ice cream mustache!
TOSS!
See?

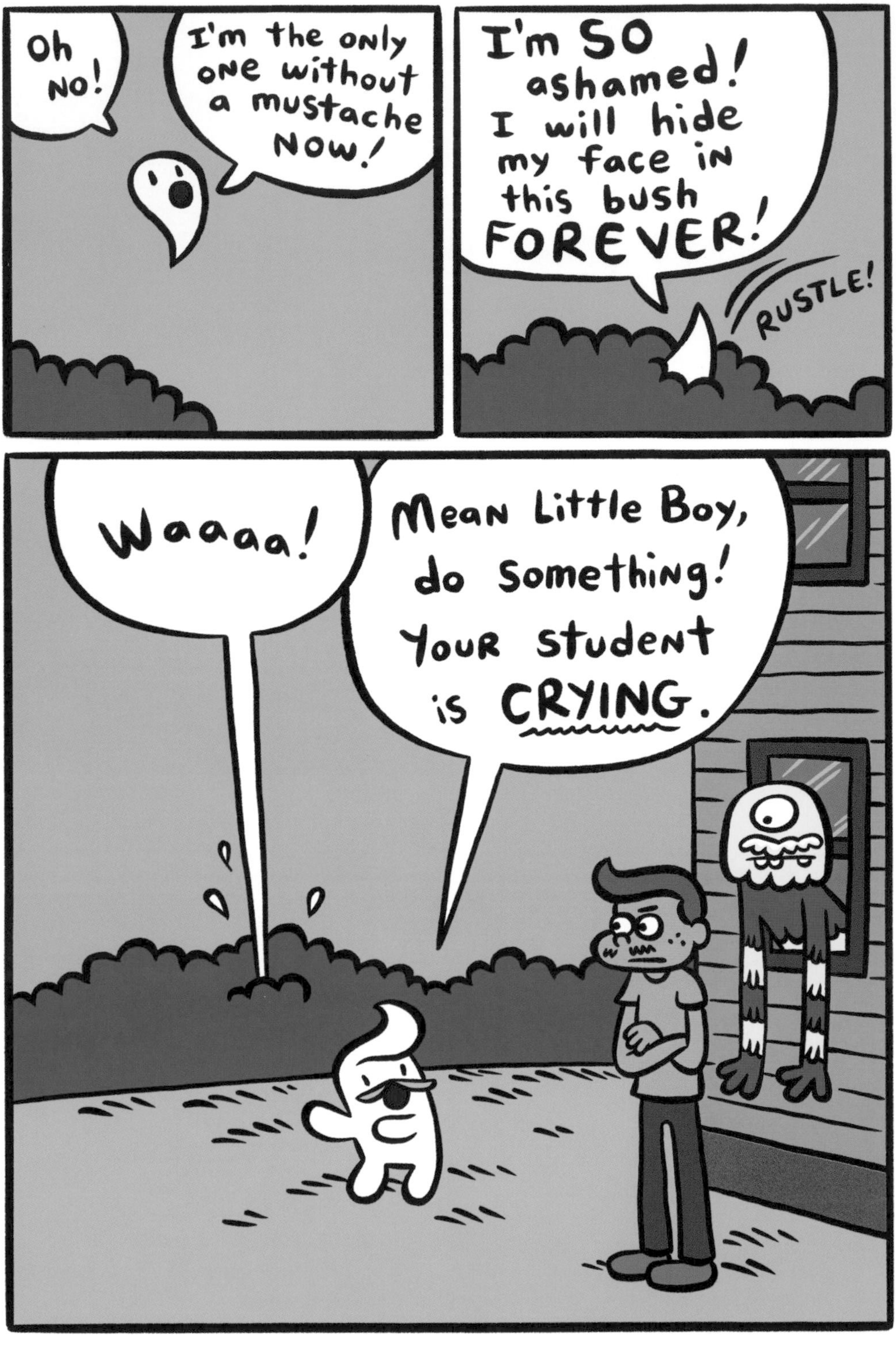

Oh NO!
I'm the only one without a mustache NOW!
I'm SO ashamed! I will hide my face in this bush FOREVER!
RUSTLE!
Waaaa!
Mean Little Boy, do Something! Your student is CRYING.

CHAPTER SEVEN

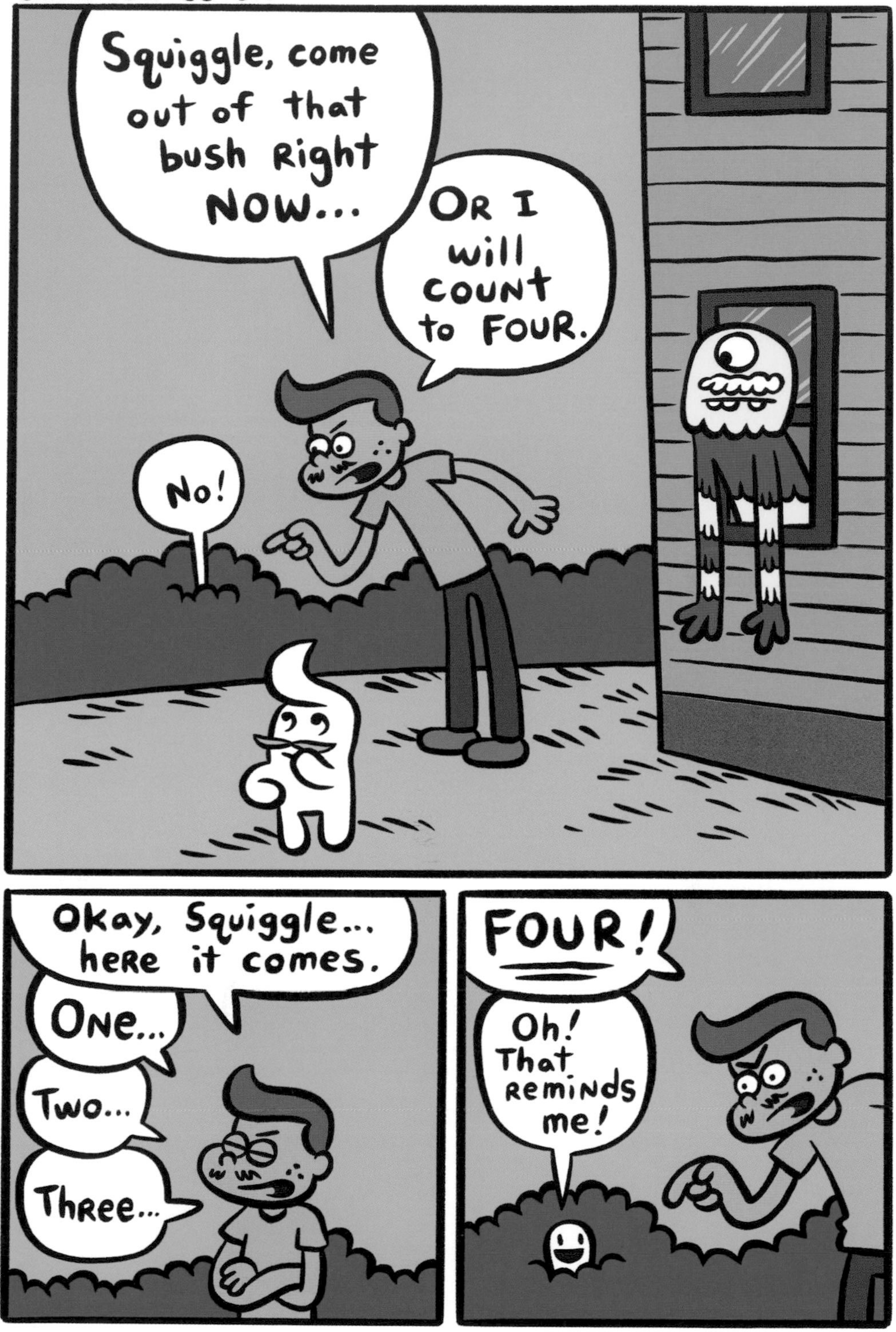
Squiggle, come out of that bush Right NOW...
OR I will COUNT to FOUR.
No!
Okay, Squiggle... here it comes.
ONE...
Two...
Three...
FOUR!
Oh! That Reminds me!

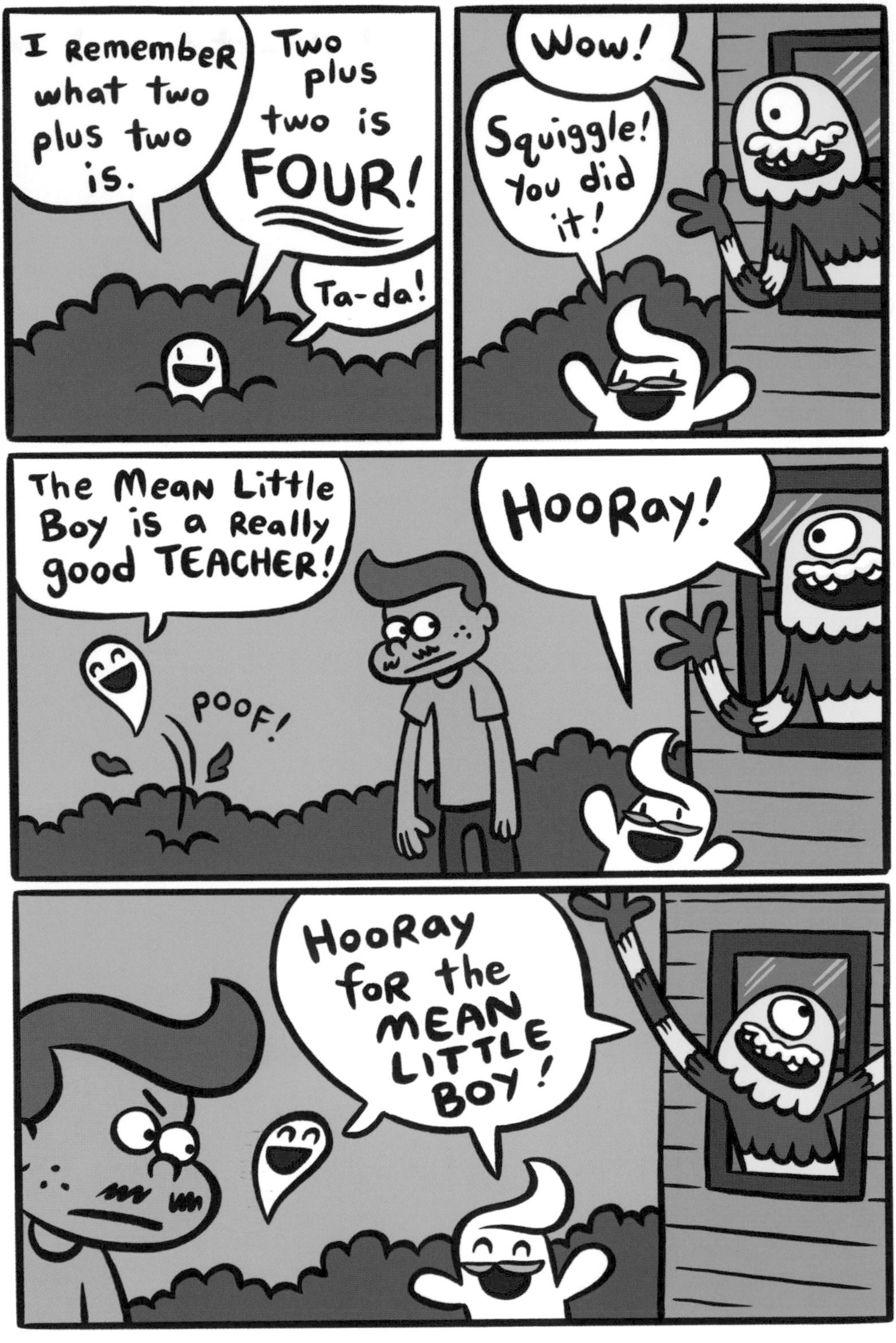
I remember what two plus two is.
Two plus two is FOUR!
Ta-da!
Wow!
Squiggle! You did it!
The Mean Little Boy is a really good TEACHER!
HOORAY!
POOF!
HOORAY for the MEAN LITTLE BOY!

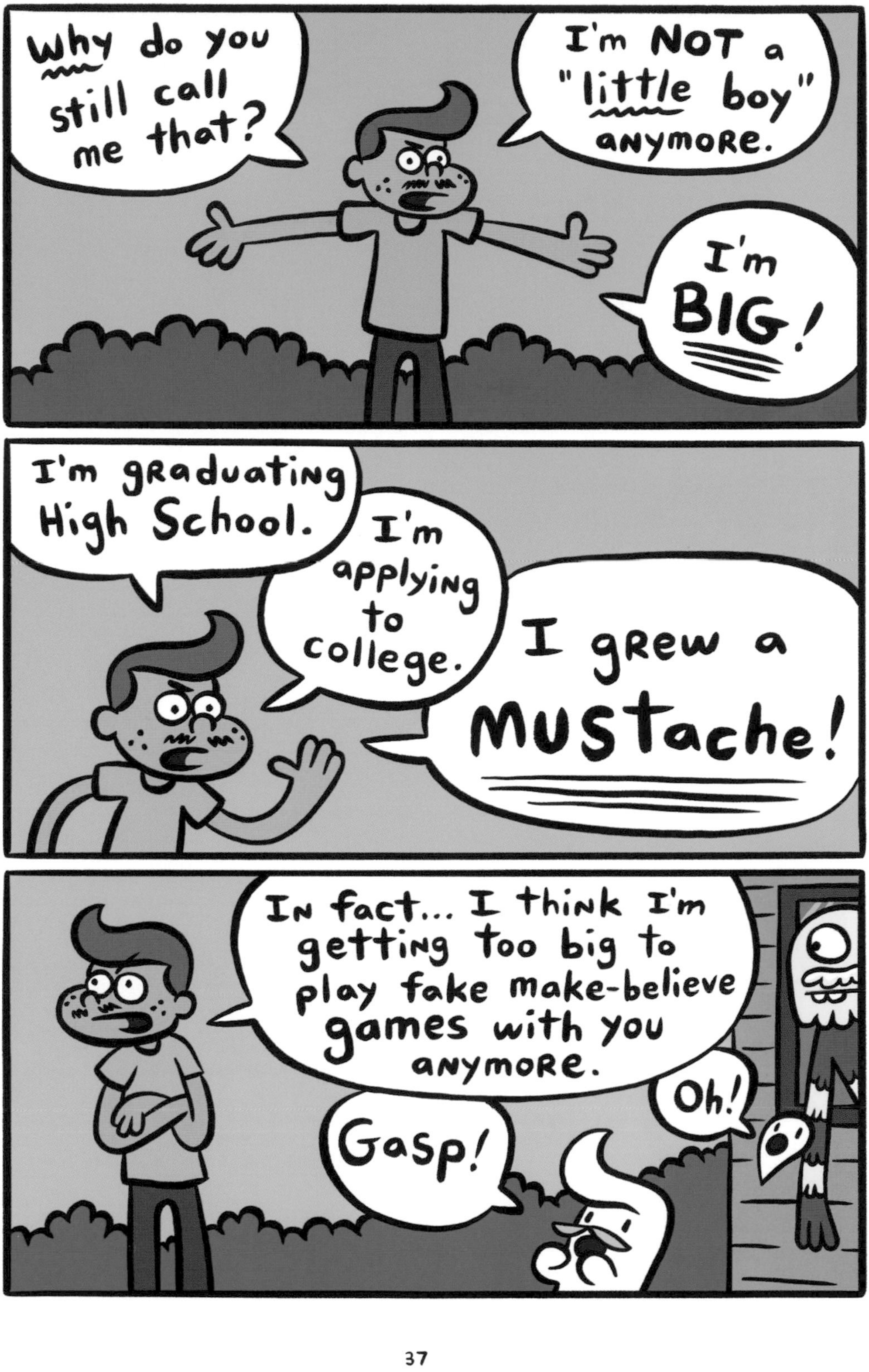
Why do you still call me that?
I'm NOT a "little boy" anymore.
I'm BIG!
I'm graduating High School.
I'm applying to college.
I grew a MUSTache!
In fact... I think I'm getting too big to play fake make-believe games with you anymore.
Gasp!
Oh!

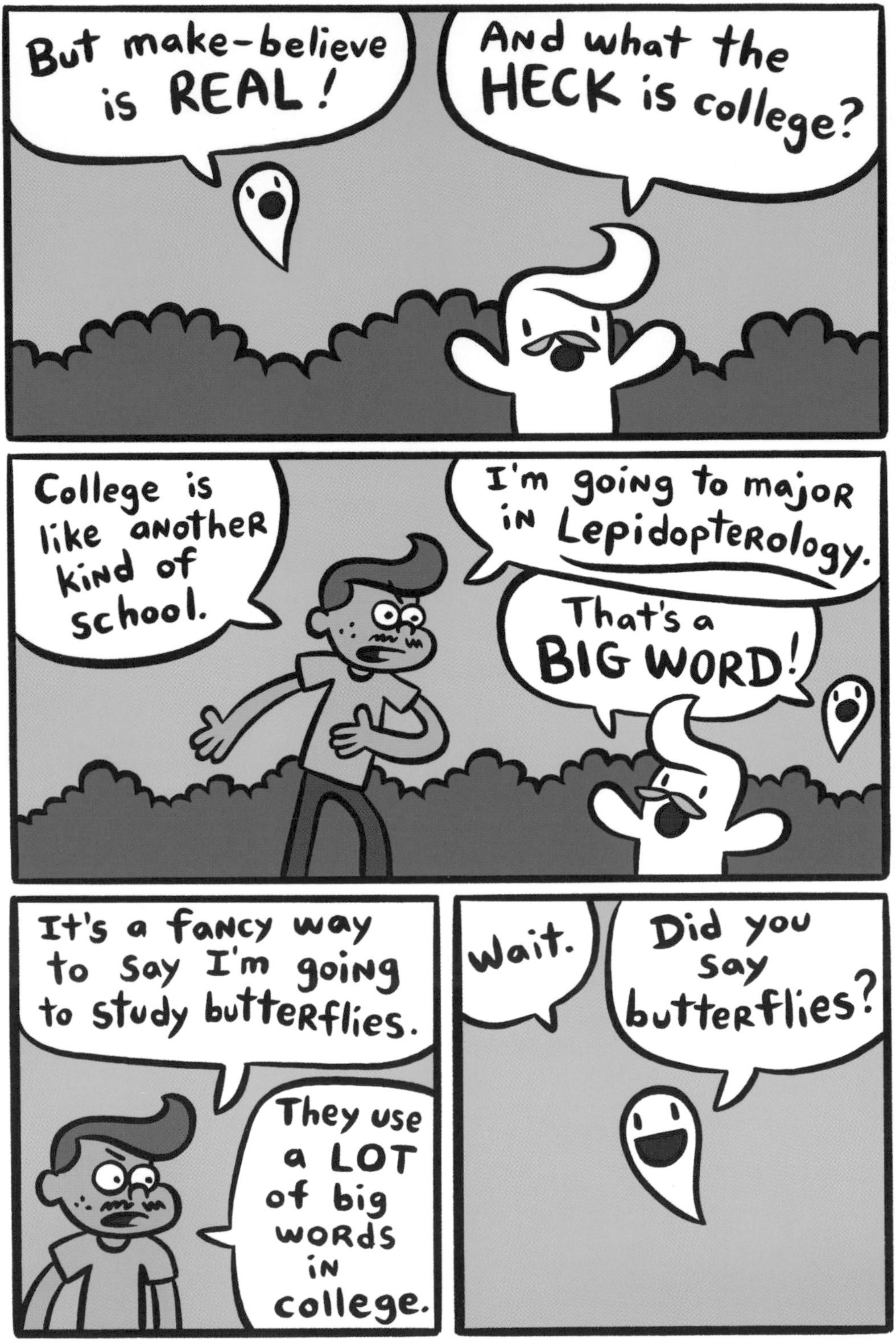
But make-believe is REAL!
And what the HECK is college?
College is like another kind of school.
I'm going to major in Lepidopterology.
That's a BIG WORD!
It's a fancy way to say I'm going to study butterflies.
They use a LOT of big words in college.
Wait.
Did you say butterflies?

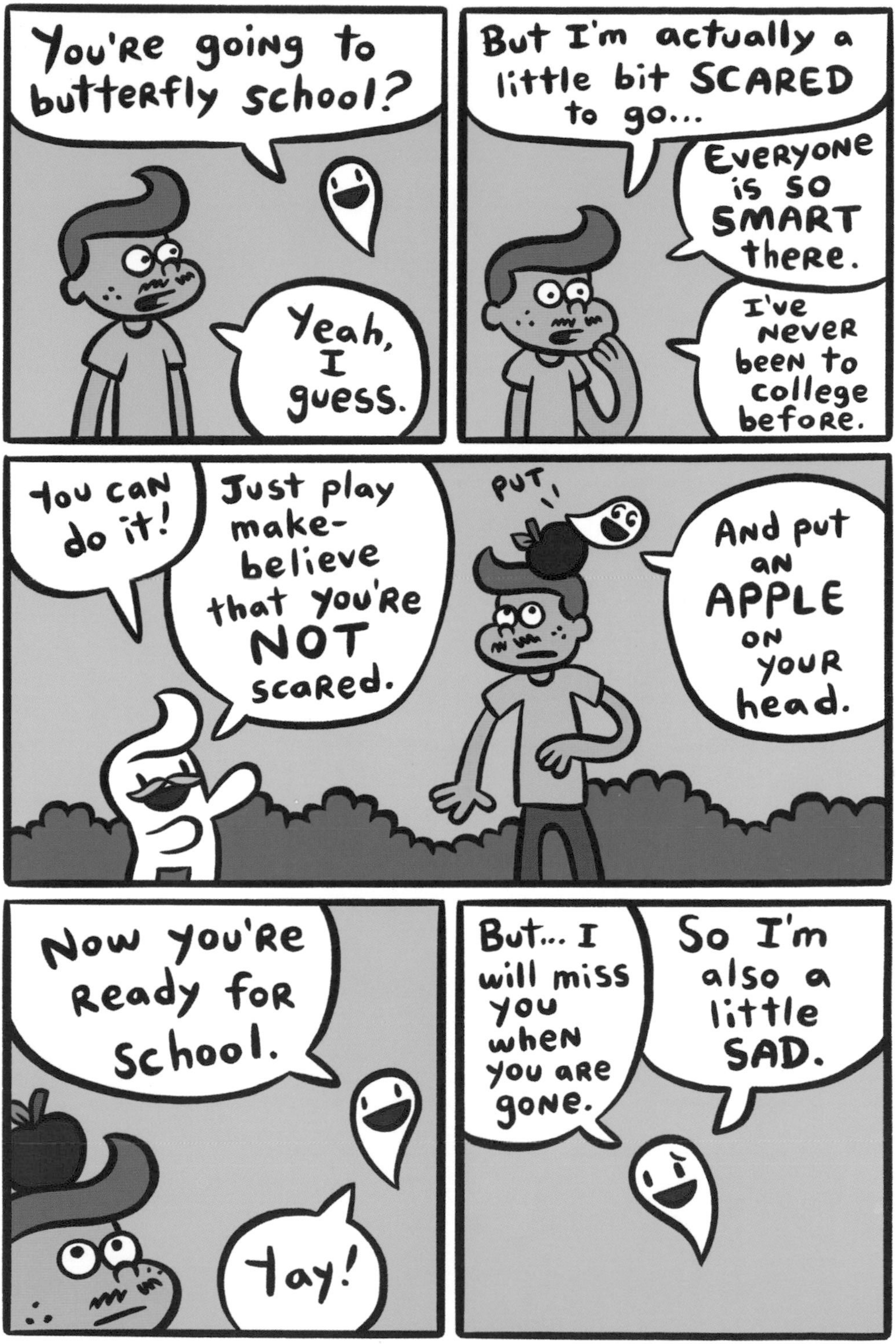
You're going to butterfly school?
Yeah, I guess.
But I'm actually a little bit SCARED to go...
Everyone is so SMART there.
I've never been to college before.
You can do it!
Just play make-believe that you're NOT scared.
PUT
And put an APPLE on your head.
Now you're ready for school.
Yay!
But... I will miss you when you are gone.
So I'm also a little SAD.

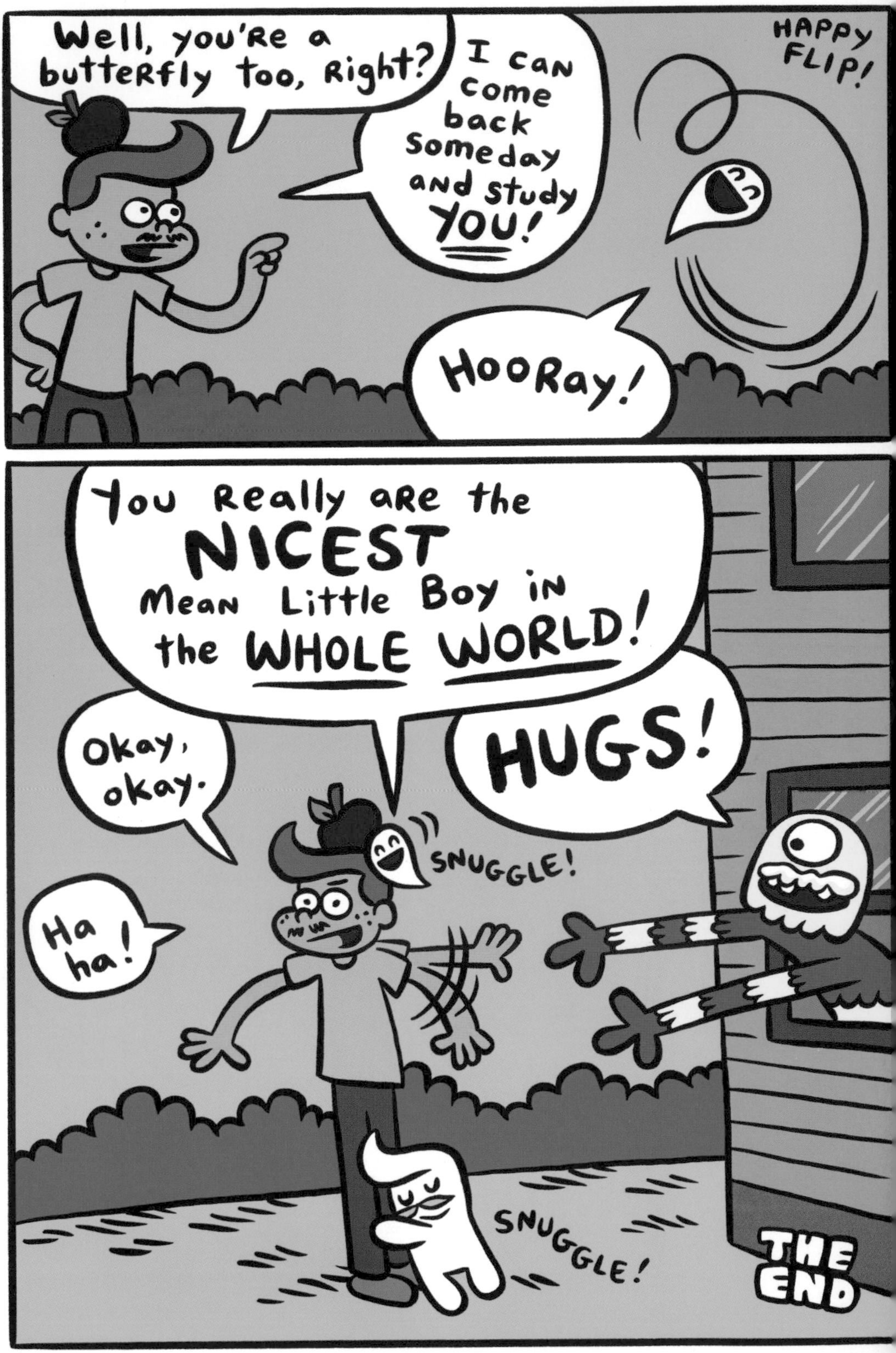
Well, you're a butterfly too, right?
I can come back someday and study YOU!
HAPPY FLIP!
HOORay!
You really are the NICEST Mean Little Boy in the WHOLE WORLD!
HUGS!
Okay, okay.
SNUGGLE!
Ha ha!
SNUGGLE!
THE END